I0620734

SEAN CUMMINGS

THE CANADIAN

WEREWOLF

CHRONICLE

STORIES FROM WITNESSES TO THE WEREWOLF PHENOMENON.

THE CANADIAN WEREWOLF CHRONICLE

Stories From Witnesses To The Werewolf Phenomenon

SEAN CUMMINGS

BACK ALLEY BOOKS

Copyright © 2022 Sean Cummings

All rights reserved

The characters and events portrayed in this book are fictitious. Any similarity to real persons, living or dead, is coincidental and not intended by the author.

No part of this book may be reproduced, or stored in a retrieval system, or transmitted in any form or by any means, electronic, mechanical, photocopying, recording, or otherwise, without express written permission of the publisher.

CONTENTS

For Jack Pierce.

ABOUT WEREWOLVES AND OTHER SCARY THINGS

Everybody has a favorite monster. For some it is an enormous shark. For others it's a mummy or a vampire. For me, it's always going to be a werewolf. Ever since I was a kid and watched Henry Hull's *Werewolf of London*. Scared the living hell out of me. And then *The Wolfman* and Lon Chaney's excellent performance as the tortured Larry Talbot. The incredible makeup by Jack Pierce in both cases.

So, let's just imagine if these things were real? What if raw, bestial howling filled the air beneath the light of a full moon? Now imagine being stalked by a creature that resembles a wolf but is as large as a full-grown brown bear. A creature with a face and fangs out of your worst nightmare. A beast that only knows hunting and killing in the most savage manner possible.

City, town, or village, rural or in the north, a monster is hungry, and you might be on the menu.

Just imagine ... What would witnesses say about what they've just seen? What might survivors of a werewolf attack have to say knowing that they themselves will become a monster? And what about science? Is there any data on a phenomenon that no scholar or scientist can even agree exists?

Is there legal standing for a creature that only lives and breathes for a few hours each month? What about the legal standing of the human hosting the monster? How far might government go to hide evidence that werewolves existed? Are there stories from the past about the monsters? How could folklore become blood-soaked fact? Where do werewolves come from in the first place? (Lots of speculation on that one.)

In this volume, I've envisioned a world where such terrifying creatures exist. Where there is no place to hide once the werewolf catches your scent. Whether it's Canada's Atlantic provinces or Vancouver Island. From Whistler Mountain to Winnipeg. From Capreol to Rivière-du-Loup. A monster is on the loose. It hasn't eaten for a month and will kill everything in its path.

This is an expert hunter, and it will not be denied. It doesn't matter if the prey is human, Hereford or even another pack of wolves.

So, here is my invitation to you: let's explore what it might be like to live in a world where these monsters are on the hunt whenever there is a full moon. Where a dead terrifying howl fills the midnight sky and smart people stay in the house behind locked doors.

Sean Cummings - January 2022

INTRODUCTION

I saw a wolf on the side of the highway once. I was driving between Winnipeg and Brandon Manitoba. It was fucking huge. That (brief) encounter was one of the foundations of my wanting to write fantasy stories set in Manitoba. The moment was one of my first inklings that anything could be out there, lurking in the wilds once you leave the city lights. When I told the story to friends or strangers, everyone insisted it was probably just a dog. Or a coyote. I've seen dogs. I've seen coyotes. And I know a motherfucking wolf when I see one. I know the feeling of seeing something you weren't prepared to see.

It's never quite left me. The sensation was startlingly similar to when a dog you didn't see growls and lunges at you while you're out for a walk. You were safe, and then it's there. Right. There. It's close. Too close. Did you see a fence? Will that stop it? What I felt when I saw that wolf was that chill, magnified. I had a car around me, and I was traveling at highway speed, and still that wolf sticks with me. That's the power and mystique they hold.

As cool as real wolves are, because I'm a fantasy and horror fan, I love their mythic cousins even more. Werewolves are awesome in pretty much any of their incarnations, from Lon Chaney in *The Wolfman* to the *Werewolf* TV show from the 80s, to *True Blood*. I've played the *Werewolf the Apocalypse* roleplaying game (when will you rage?) and I've had a *Dungeons & Dragons* character turned into a werewolf (tragically cured of the affliction, because my friends knew that I always roll gangbusters when "forced" into attacking the party). I've read werewolf detectives in urban fantasy and sexy shifters in paranormal romance. I've followed comic characters like Bigby Wolf in *Fables*, and, of course, good old Jack Russell, Marvel's *Werewolf by Night*.

I love a good werewolf movie (and if you follow me on Twitter, you'll quickly see I also love a *bad* werewolf movie too). From Warren Zevon's "Werewolves of London" to the Tragically Hip's "I'm a Werewolf, Baby," I've filled playlists of lycanthropic mood music and homebrewed soundtracks. When Marvel Studios announced the *Moon Knight* TV show, I immediately began crossing my fingers and toes for a Werewolf by Night spinoff. But of all its incarnations, my absolute favourite version of the werewolf is the wolf-man engine of destruction and terror. The primal blend of the best and worst of civilization and nature. I *still* have the classic Universal Studios Wolfman action figure my grandma bought me in a variety store in a small town near my old home.

Sean and I tend to respond to all of each other's werewolf-related social media posts, so I've been following *The Canadian Werewolf Chronicle* come together for some time. To say I've been looking forward to reading it is an understatement. An authoritative journalistic expose of the real werewolf problem? I haven't seen that before, so how could I pass it up? I'm thrilled Sean trusted me with an early reading copy and asked me to write this introduction. In the ongoing hellscape of 2021 and beyond, why couldn't werewolves be real? And if they are, maybe howling at the moon will bring us all some relief.

The Canadian Werewolf Chronicle brings together found evidence in journals and date books, accounts from animal rights activists, consultants, scientists, government, and law enforcement officials—all anonymous of course—and yes, stories from the teeth of the werewolves themselves. Is *The Canadian Werewolf Chronicle* a compelling tale of a horror that might be, or a dire warning of what is?

With a modern Kolchak narrator, and a terrifying Canada full of monsters for him to chase, the question hangs over the entire book: what is waiting for a humanity that has stopped fearing the supernatural? Do you dare to find out? Read along with me, friends, and tell me, will you cower at the coming of the night, or will you bark at the moon?

Chadwick Ginther - December 2021

PROTECT YOURSELF! STAY ALIVE!

The Werewolf Phenomenon is real. Non-belief in werewolves will not protect you. There is no werewolf atheism. The monsters exist north of the 49th parallel, and they thrive in sub-zero cold and deep snow, so don't think that Canada's long, miserable winters will save you. Cities, towns, villages; the range of the Canadian Werewolf is everywhere human beings are found.

Officials will say that werewolves don't exist, so, they stonewall and redact. Werewolves are here. Right now. If you're in the wrong place at the wrong time you can count on being ripped to pieces in short order. For a small measure of that time, you will still be alive as the monster feeds. When the creature is done its grisly business, all that will be left of you is a shredded mass of freshly dead meat. Exposed ribs silhouetted against the moonlit sky. Torn and twitching muscle tissue, organs, crushed bones.

Folklore going back more than a thousand years speaks of shape shifting creatures. In the medieval world, a strange species known as Dog Heads were said to exist and even lived in their own villages. These strange creatures should be listed in the archaeological record somewhere but forget about it. You won't find werewolf fossils either because, officially, such creatures cannot exist.

Werewolves cannot be real and yet must be.

They are here in the north.

It should be common knowledge: that each full moon a human host will completely transform in mind, body, and soul. They quite terrifyingly become another creature entirely – and it is a wholesale transformation. Nothing is left of the human being. It can take up to an excruciating thirty minutes to complete the change and for at least part of that time, the creature's host can feel his or her bones snapping and reshaping. Their heart enlarging. Lungs. Claws tearing through fingertips.

The creature, now fully transformed, is as large as a sub-compact automobile. The moon has done its work, and the creature covets the night the way a beggar covets a twenty-dollar bill. It knows its time to hunt is short. Woe to the poor soul or dumb forest animal that lands the attention of its hypersensitive hearing or a nose that can pick up a man's scent from miles away.

Over the years, there have been numerous accounts of monsters that hunt in the wild forests of northern Canada. Wolf-like creatures that feast on moose, or elk or deer. Sometimes the partially eaten carcass of a brown bear is found. One night a month. Twelve times a year. Nothing is safe. If your heart pumps warm blood and you happen to be in werewolf country during a full moon, start running. Run for your blessed life. Because it knows you are here, and it is stalking you. It hears the twigs snapping as you stagger, terrified through the twisted undergrowth. The beast isn't far behind, and your time is up. Your life will end in terror and gore.

The monsters tear through the shadows on four legs, though, on occasion, they will appear as bipedal. Some believe a two-legged werewolf must mean the creature's hold on the host has been weakened somehow. That the man or woman inside is fighting to come out. (I'm not sure anyone tested this theory.) Fully transformed, a great thick mane of silver-gray fur surrounds its neck, shoulders, and chest. Its glowing eyes are a pair of burning coals set deep inside a skull that is hard as granite. A wild face. Feral. Hungry. Calculating. A mouth full of gleaming white teeth like that of the Hyena except longer and sharper. A snout that can sniff out a pin drop of blood in a fountain of water.

A madman. An escaped lunatic. That's how a werewolf attack will be dismissed when it's the first instance. Only after a few more full moons when authorities realize no human being could render wounds on the victims with such savagery do they consider what their logical minds won't allow. In the next breath, unfortunately, it is explained away as a wild animal of some kind – a bear perhaps? A mountain lion? (Wait a minute. Wasn't the latest victim found on the eighteenth floor of an office building? Lots of wild animals in office buildings these days.)

Indeed, the mere notion that a human being can transform into another creature entirely, most often a wolf, is still scoffed at by most rational people. This is completely understandable as denial is the first line of defense. For many, a kind of tunnel vision sets in afterward.

Some rely on recipes that are half-baked folklore and half dumb luck to protect themselves and their loved ones. Runes carved into a doorway. Pagan spells buried all over one's property because you can't be sure of the direction the beast will be coming from. Magic circles surrounding the house. Crucifixes. (Wrong monster.) Cold iron. (Wrong monster again.)

Of course, there is always silver, the old lie.

Any metal jacketed high caliber bullet will do the trick. The creature has enhanced healing but nowhere enough reserve when it is full of holes. Bludgeoning works but is rare as human beings can count on having their own head torn off if within reach of the monster's claws. If you somehow manage to take the creature's head off, it will be dead. Some orders have shadowy men and women who carry swords blessed by the heads of all the world's major religions. They are expert when it comes to tracking and killing the beasts. Cutting the bloodline. Cutting the possibility of future massacres out of the picture entirely.

As mentioned, there are few who believe in such things. It is usually the unbeliever who winds up as werewolf chow. Believers know better than to escort their significant others through a park beneath the light of a full moon. Werewolf attacks always, always, always happen just off the path inside a city park.

Canadians number somewhere between thirty and forty million souls. Here it is cold, mostly. Here is where the land is blanketed in starch white snow from October right on through to the beginning of April. Where the east coast sea churns up waves tall as office buildings and where wind and ice-cold rain batters those on the boats as well as on the docks. Here also is where the land is so flat that one is but a speck in a yellow golden field of canola. But here is where there exist towering mountain ranges stretching the length of the continent. Where the sting of frostbite and the crunch of sub-zero snow beneath your feet are your constant companion for months on end.

A bit of old and new technology. I have observed raw footage of these creatures, caught on CCTV. I have interviewed a police officer whose body camera contained footage of one of the creatures as it fed. Three shots from the officer's .357 Magnum and the creature lay dead beside its prey, back in a bloodied human form. I have also seen the written gag order the officer lives under since the authorities will no doubt have seen the body camera footage and will have made up their minds for themselves.

I have witnessed footage of a boy in a locked panic room transform into a monster. A specially designed space that had triple grade industrial rebar woven into a tight mesh prior to the concrete being poured. Heavy steel reinforcement including a blast and fire-proof door. The child, incidentally, was not bitten by a werewolf and survived. At age six, according to his engineer father, the boy transformed for the first time and butchered the family dog. A mutation? Possibly. Research is needed and of course, a willing subject.

I have puzzled over several questions: is a werewolf a true species if only for one night a month? Is this phenomenon proof of another form of human evolution? Is there any other creature in the animal kingdom which possesses the ability to change its entire biology? If so, where does this lead our species? And what of the human soul? Does it cease to be during the time the full moon is calling the shots? If werewolves are real, surely God must also be real. So argues a host in one of the stories I have collected. If God is therefore real, then so must the Devil.

Of course, much depends on an individual's interpretation of a supreme being. But what if we were to somehow separate the religious elements which exist in werewolf folklore from what we know about the creatures in the here and now. It is not a dark curse that forces the transformation during the full moon. Transformation is, I believe, an extremely rare phenomenon that is worthy of serious scientific research.

To date, no-one has successfully hunted a werewolf and taken it *down with tranquilizer darts. Perhaps the first order of business after accepting the reality of werewolves in our midst, is to acknowledge that as rare as a werewolf attack might be, you can count on the occasional survivor who got away from the monster with only slight wounds. Those people must be found quickly and helped. That must be the starting point in understanding these creatures.*

As a final note, the truth of these monstrous predators must already be known by those in the corridors of power. Now that U.S. intelligence has submitted a report stating that "UAP (Unidentified Aerial Phenomenon) clearly pose a safety of flight issue and may pose a challenge to U.S. national security"—anything goes now.

What do I believe? What do <u>you</u> believe? That's the only thing that matters,
frankly. For this author, the creatures must be real. Even if you don't believe, have a mind for your safety on those full-moon nights. Lock your doors and windows and bring the family dog inside. Fido is usually the first to go when a werewolf visits the suburbs, so, for God's sake, don't leave your dog out as bait. Listen to the sounds of the night. Familiarize yourself with the sounds of your dwelling and the street outside during the silent hours.

Sleep with one eye open one night a month. Protect yourself and those you love. If you choose to believe, of course.

CHAPTER 1: THE WEREWOLF PHENOMENON IS REAL

The Werewolf Phenomenon—it's an actual thing. For the authorities, it is getting harder and harder to cover up the existence of these creatures because of mankind's technological leap forward. If UAP's can be real and pose a national security threat, then why not the existence of werewolves?

And if werewolves exist, what else might there be? What kinds of threats do they pose? What causes them to exist in the first place? (One colleague thinks there is a climate change connection.) I could come up with dozens of questions but to answer them, I must also believe that werewolves are real. It does feel very much like we are just scratching the surface of the extent of the phenomenon.

It Doesn't Care What You Believe

"I've been a host to a werewolf now for five years. Brutal attack back in Winnipeg. It made the news. Six dead with yours truly as the only survivor. Flash forward to now: I haven't killed anyone yet ... or the monster hasn't. I call it The Werewolf of Winnipeg because, duh. The reason is the thing that killed my friends and left me alive with huge scars across my chest was a fucking werewolf. They shot the thing and it turned out to be some old woman who lived alone with her cats.

I know that if you survive an attack, according to folklore, you will become a werewolf next full moon. That monster was the biggest wolf I'd ever seen. I wouldn't even call it a complete wolf. Its claws were half-human. There was a locket hanging from a chain on the goddamned thing.

I didn't question it. My survival meant that I had to do something to make myself safe during the full moon. I won't tell you what I do and where I go because it is my secret and if you knew about it you would do something stupid like go out there next full moon and set up a camera. I know what I become. I don't feel cursed. I am doing everything I can do to keep myself safe from you and you from me. I am not ashamed of it. I feel robbed of what most people would classify as a normal life. But I know what I become is truly a monster and I don't want anyone's death by my hands.

It doesn't care what you believe, the wolf. It doesn't give three shits what kind of car you drive or whether you're a rich asshole or a desperate beggar. I possess no memories of what my monster does on full-moon nights. I can piece it together quite quickly the morning after a change. In a lot of cases I can follow the wolf's tracks from the night before. But no, I haven't killed a human being. I have no intention of killing a human being. I also have no intention of ending my life to end the curse. I don't owe anybody nothing."

The Authorities Hands Are Tied

"I'm retired now so they can't do anything to me to keep my mouth shut. I worked for forty years in the administrative side of local government. My job was to provide clerical support, so, I said little but listened a lot. We ladies were a good bunch to work with. Never a severe problem keeping the lid on the big secret because we all knew what was at stake if the truth ever got out. (And I think it will. I mean, it's starting to happen. Slowly.)

I ran the administrative team in the Deputy Mayor's office, that's as high as I went. Being an Alderman, the Deputy Mayor wore two hats at city council meetings. It's a tough job, city council. Tougher still when everyone on the team is trying their level best to convince the public that a wild animal was responsible for the recent attacks. (Particularly handy excuse when someone uploads video of a creature onto social media.) That or the 'wild man' explanation. They will often haul out an 'expert' on mental illness. Anything to make that horrifying scene from last night disappear from the public's consciousness quickly as possible.

They all knew about it and I'm not defending their silence or manipulation of the facts in telling the truth about the creatures, but you must understand that the authorities' hands are tied. If the Mayor or the Chief of Police, for example, were to let slip those local authorities are in possession of proof of existence: Hair with unrecognizable DNA. CCTV. Body camera footage. Photographs. Audio. Unnaturally large dog or wolf prints. If that gets out people lose it. Forget about the danger werewolves present, City Hall worries about the dangers humans present to each other if the thin veil of control dissolves into anarchy. These days it sure does feel like that veil of control is getting thinner and thinner.

And there are legal questions, too. Say the police take in a naked guy covered in human blood. The blood comes from a pair of mutilated late-night joggers the cops found in the park. There are giant wolf prints all around the bodies. There are deep gouging wounds that could only be made by something with claws and not fingernails.

The only evidence they have to show that the naked guy might be the killer is the blood from the bodies. But … where are the human footprints at the murder scene? I mean, beyond that of the joggers? You see, they have to use the wild man excuse and they pretend the physical evidence of a werewolf doesn't exist. Stick to script. Deny, deny, deny. No journalist who wishes to keep his or her job in a media market where print journalism is on life support will want to cover the physical evidence. Because werewolves can't be real. They just can't."

We Need to Study the Creature

"Truth eventually comes to light. I mean, from official sources. I teach Philosophy, Culture and Religion at the local university. This is my fourteenth year. I'm multi-published. I've won a couple of awards.

Still, there is nothing in my toolbox of human understanding that offers me any greater insight into werewolves, their prevalence, and the threat they pose. I've not yet taken time to contemplate deeper meanings such as who is responsible for killing and maiming people if the human hosting the creature truly ceases to exist for a handful of hours each month beneath a full moon. That person ceases to be, don't they?

Does the human hosting the creature owe something to the greater community? If so, what is that something? Who dares go there? For me, hosts need our help. We need to study the creature in a secure, escape-proof environment. We need to apply the scientific method to unlock the secrets of this savage change. Study ... not dissect. There is nothing that can be found in the human body that would prove the existence of two species at once. There is no 'inner wolf.' There is no wild creature lurking beneath the host's skin.

And yet, I have witnessed a terrifyingly complete transformation. An achingly slow process where bones snap and reform. Where flesh is remolded into something large, powerful, and hungry. Where the beast moves with speed far beyond the scope of the human eye. It exists to hunt, kill, and feed. Over and over and over, for as long as possible during its one night of existence each month.

My eyes, my intellect, my philosophical center told me that what I was seeing could not be real. But it was real. It was the most frightening creature I've ever laid eyes on. Long and strong. Tall at the shoulder. A wolf's legs, feet, and tail. The face of a Devil. The face of an immediate, horrifyingly brutal death. This was the Capreol creature for anyone who might be interested. They brought the man in after finding him covered with a murder victim's blood. He was also nude. This was first thing in the morning. He was brought in processed and put into the justice system. He turned into a wolf awaiting a preliminary hearing and killed ten prisoners and two guards before they shot the creature dead. I saw the monster. I saw what it did. They smuggled out the security footage. My eyes told me it couldn't be real. It was.

I had to process that. We all have much to process as the truth trickles out. Human hosts need to know they can be safely studied. That's all I have to say about it. The creatures are real, and I am growing to accept the new reality."

Something About Moonlight Flips a Switch on Evolution

"What we're undoubtedly looking at is something evolutionary. A fascinating and terrifying new branch of life that must be studied further. I'm a biologist, and what I have been asked to investigate would normally be classified as arcane. It's not. These creatures exist and wreak havoc in our world for the briefest of periods. Something about moonlight flips a switch on evolution. How can moonlight act as a catalyst for a wholesale transformation from one species into another species. One that doesn't technically exist because werewolves can't be real. They're folklore, right?

Unfortunately, our institutions aren't equipped to manage this revelation. There is a purposeful culture of secrecy around unnatural occurrences inside government at every level. I've seen this deliberate attempt to stifle the truth in action. Because to speak of this phenomenon as to be real is a kind of heresy to what we already know about evolution and why there is life on this planet.

I am always questioning because the existence of werewolves points to a need for a wholesale review of how science looks at evolutionary biology. I along with a small handful of scientists who believe in the werewolf phenomenon are asking the questions that need to be asked.

One of our groups is a theoretical physicist who believes human beings are vessels which act as gateway into our plane of existence that can only be unlocked by a full moon's light. That obviously sounds far-fetched, I get that. But what we know about the universe could be contained on the head of a pin compared to that which we haven't yet discovered. An open mind is necessary.

I have not shared the same space as a host during a full moon.

There are organizations which exist to create a safe space for hosts where their condition can run its course in a controlled environment each month. I have witnessed three transformations. Each time, a similar creature in size and facial features. Almost as if the human part of the transformation refused to give into the wolf and what we're left with is a terrifying human-wolf face. A long snout. A maw full of sharp teeth. Long sharp teeth.

Valid criticism suggests that such events are concocted events using man-made special effects. There is no biological change. It's a scam. But what about the physical evidence of the presence of these creatures in our world? Bits of fur. Enormous footprints.

Non-human victims. Human or non-huma, the same kinds of death scenes each time. An orgy of violence and gore. Tissue damage so severe that it could only have come from an enormous apex predator. That's it. That's all.

Listen, it's an open secret that a wild man cannot be the culprit each time a mutilated and partially eaten human corpse is found the morning after a full moon. The lack of open dialogue on the subject gives one the feeling that our elected ones need to close ranks and stonewall. They know we know they are lying. But to tell the truth? Where might that lead?

Where does the creature go when the full moon is over? The host dissolves back into human form. Where is the animal? This fiercest of predators? Where does this terrifying hunter disappear to when the sun comes up?

Either the creatures have always been with us (which I am inclined to believe since we haven't yet found biological life anywhere but Earth.) or we are dealing with something new, terrifying, and important. Our initial reaction is to destroy such beasts on sight. Even with modern weapons, thermal imagery, drones, and satellite technology, werewolves are masters of the night. They are hard to see until it's too late. I suspect that as technology improves, so too will footage of the beasts.

Just saying those words, 'the beasts.' It feels so Victorian. Nevertheless, the human being is no longer present in the physical sense or psychological sense. That's the amazing feature of this terrifying phenomenon: complete transmogrification. And here we are, a scientific world in possession of the tools necessary to investigate the creature further if we only choose to do so. Are we prepared to study it, or should we pretend it doesn't exist?

Much religion and superstition are tied up in our collective response to the truth that werewolves exist. It's easy to believe in werewolf curses or doomed bloodlines. It's easy to believe that savage murder in your neighborhood last night was perpetrated by a madman.

It is a lot harder to accept that something exists with a taste for human flesh and that you might not even be safe in your own house because the creature can also become bipedal at will. Like, maybe the monster is channeling the human being host because it can then walk like us and tear fleshy things apart with its forepaws.

Not enough has been said about the creature's teeth. There are many in the animal kingdom with terrifying looking teeth. One immediately thinks of a shark with its rows of razor-sharp backward-pointing teeth. The ultimate predator. But there are other creatures in existence just as frightening? That's what I would like to know. No doubt some kind of clash between the dominant species, I suspect. Them versus Us."

Government Knows More Than They Are Letting On

"They make you sign non-disclosure agreements when you start work with the government. It doesn't matter what level. I think it's hard to be anything but skeptical when it comes to werewolves or the phenomenon as they are now calling it. But isn't that the job of government? To be skeptical and to keep a lid on anything that will blow the voting public's mind?

Werewolves fit neatly into the mind-blowing category. My late wife and were investigating what local government knew about a series of gruesome unsolved killings dating back five years. Each victim was murdered on the night of a full moon and each body utterly destroyed by a monster which somehow exists when it shouldn't. Does that make sense?

Between the crime scene photos and witness statements, the hard evidence. Six separate killings in the span a year and a half. A lull of seven months, cumulative, and then three more killings going back five years. Always the same stonewalling answer from police and local authorities: wild man or wild animal is the perpetrator. To hell with what the security footage once said because it's gone baby, gone. They disappear the physical evidence.

Where to? *(He shrugs.)* A warehouse maybe? An old potash mine near Moose Jaw? I've never thought government to be that clever, so, I suspect there is an arm's length agency that cleans up evidence of a supernatural being that should not exist yet does. My wife and I collected two boxes full of redacted official documents courtesy of freedom of information requests that I continue to make. Each document covered with black marks. Covering up the truth.

What's at stake?

This is a monster that hunts the most vulnerable in our city. The homeless and the mentally ill. People forced to work ungodly hours because they are newcomers to Canada. Life isn't kind to people on the bottom of the socio-economic scale most days. Now they have to worry about being eaten by a huge predator. The rich can afford gated communities I suppose. Not that a werewolf gives three shits about where its victims reside.

The truth needs to come out, but I don't hold any hope of an end to the stonewalling. There is a lot at stake if the government held a news conference to announce that werewolves were real and here's the proof—can you imagine how the public would react? People lose their minds over wearing masks in a pandemic and now you go and tell everyone they are suddenly a food group? Government must lie because that is what governments do. The only difference between lying about a pair of mutilated street people and lying about a hidden tax increase is the subject matter. That's it. Politicians are built to lie and obfuscate. Because ... they have to. They absolutely must keep lying to us. Government knows more than they are letting on about a lot of things. Werewolves are just another 'thing' on their list to lie to us about.

I get that civil society is just a thin veneer. Government needs to give citizens a sense that all is well. All is under control when it very clearly is not. Truth needs to see the light of day and people must make up their minds for themselves despite the threat against control and civil power.

I'll finish of by saying that it's not just our government here at home. These creatures appear every full moon all over the globe. How many are there? I can't say for certain because my only unit of measurement are headlines relating to murder victims having been torn to pieces. I search using the keywords wild man or wild animal attack. It's speculative but it's just one way of connecting the dots to get a sense of how prevalent the werewolf phenomenon is."

Is There Any Humanity Left Inside?

Author's Note: Below is a journal entry from 1912. It is unique for two reasons: it was written by a person who was hunting a werewolf and it describes very briefly how the creature attacked him and how he survived.

April 17, 1912:

I have questions but none can answer. Today, I have seen what shouldn't exist. The beast was savagery incarnate. It had butchered seven of our cattle. No more horrific scene could be imagined. We hunted the wolf on horseback. Then came the godawful howling. The horses spooked and sent us tumbling. Took a while to get them back and settled. We pushed on. My partner in the hunt, Martin, asked me pointedly, 'is there any humanity left inside?' I remember telling him that no human being would so destroy cattle as was done here and that tonight was a Goddamned full moon.

We knew what we were after, in our minds, that is. Most likely a large dog or wolf. Of course, neither of us had ever encountered a werewolf before. We'd always known read about legends and superstitions, but an actual monster? A man utterly transformed into another creature.

Not a half-man half-wolf. Not a beast marked by Satan. Not Satan himself. He transformed from a wolf back into a man once we shot it dead. We were bait for each other; I armed with my Remington, and Martin with a pair of six-shooters and a Remington in the saddle. Whatever came at us that night was going to have to be faster than a man scared to death can shoot.

Of course, there was no humanity left inside the creature. That's why I was determined to kill it. We followed the prints until they disappeared in waist-high wheat. This was only the second or third summer since settlers' broke ground for the first time The soil was among the most fertile, you'd find anywhere.

The tracks reappeared nearest a gully. I was ahead of Martin and the first thing the creature went for from its hiding place in the shadows. It was a flash and then another flash, from the corner of my eye. I just caught the tiniest of glimpses at it as the creature leaped at me.

It fell dead about ten feet away. The horror came next. Great gobs of fur and flesh fell off giant monster until their lay shining naked body of a man neither of us knew. Martin had put two large holes in his chest. The dead man lay on his back, the beast's claws melted away like wax. His face was serene; like he'd just stepped out of the river after seeing Jesus for the first time.

What are we to believe when men turn into wolves and who knows what else? Did God turn his back on men? The authorities were satisfied that the man had dressed in wolf's clothing to attack the sheep, or in this case, our cattle. Nothing more was said.

Monsters and mayhem. God save us all."

There Are Unnatural Beings in Existence

"Human beings are superstitious, even now well into the twenty-first century. Canada is chock-full of superstitious people – there is nothing wrong with that, frankly. An ounce of prevention. Even here in my home, the first thing you saw at my front door were the carvings in the doorframe. Each one is a protective ward against evil. Which kind of evil depends on whatever the hell shows up on my doorstep.

I don't do magic. I do cover-your-ass. Just because you might be skeptical doesn't mean I'm planning on removing the carving anytime soon. I have seen the unseeable in my line of work. (a 'consultant' was all he would offer).

Is there a magical element to the phenomenon of werewolves? What is magic, anyway? Just an undiscovered science, that's all. What I know about the world we live in is that it is not our world, not by any stretch of the imagination. Such things exist that would make a grown man like you fill your boxers. We think we know all about the natural world. We don't. There are superstitious people who, like me, take steps to protect their homes from the forces of darkness. There are unnatural beings in existence— I have seen with my own eyes.

There are living horrors out there waiting to be discovered. Werewolves are just the beginning. Their existence is not a wonder of wonders. Werewolves have always been here as long as human beings have been around. A species we know little about other than it appears one night each month to hunt and to feed. Then it disappears into its host. Are they a new species? The next rung in evolution maybe."

CHAPTER 2: HUNTER

During a full moon, there is no more dangerous creature than a werewolf. Terms like 'savage lust for human flesh' are not to be taken lightly because when the creature is hunting it won't stop until it feeds, or the first signs of dawn streak the horizon.

When you're the alpha, you're at the very top of the food chain. One in which the regular predators of the forest take a hike when they know a werewolf is in their range. The following are stories from across the country establishing the superiority of this apex predator. When the moon is full, there is no more dangerous creature walking the planet.

Story: Old Dogs

We have all heard of the 'found footage' craze in Hollywood films. What follows is found folklore. A story or an account found in the vicinity of a werewolf attack. This story was found in a partially caved-in cabin in the very north of Saskatchewan.

While there is no way to verify whether this is a true story, much of what follows sounds like it is coming from someone who is deeply familiar with the way that a man transforms into a werewolf. As a side note, I am currently researching missing American hunters in Saskatchewan going back to the province joining confederation. I feel there is more to this story yet to be revealed.

The warm mid-morning sun caressed the wrinkles on the old man's face, and he wondered, if only for a moment, whether that's what it felt like when an angel touched a person's skin. Assuming angels existed at all outside of the statues in a graveyard. He pushed a grin out from behind the thick white whiskers of a beard that had been growing since the day he started building his cabin more than forty years ago. He'd trimmed his whiskers occasionally with a pair of sharpened scissors he'd brought along with as many hand tools his duffle bag could carry.

On the other hand, it might not be long now, he mused, until he would finally see for himself whether angels were real. If so, would they also condemn a soul to hell for the terrible things he did in life while he was truly out of his mind?

Was hell even real when your very existence met the definition of the word?

"A monster exists," he said quietly. "A god so must also. But whose god? Which invisible force in the sky is it, eh? Odin? Zeus? Yahweh?"

The old man listened for a moment to see if God would answer his challenge, but it wasn't to be. He wondered, as he did every morning since he became host to the madness as a young man; how does God judge the soul of a killer if a man is made a killer? They aren't even a man anymore. And surely it was a sin to take one's own life, the good book said so. But what about those poor souls the monster slaughtered? And what about those yet to be killed if he didn't end his life, stopping the line?

"The Lord has got a great deal of answering to do," he said angrily. It came out sounding like he meant to punch the creator of all things in the face.

The old man took a deep breath of fresh air as he opened the door. His home, a small cabin nestled deep in northern Saskatchewan bush country. Crown land and a forest teaming with wildlife. Creatures he couldn't be blamed for killing when the blood in his veins turned to acid and the fever began to set in.

The sun was holy.

It was the moon that he feared most, even now at the age of eighty-one. After walking away from his love. His work. His possessions.

"But I didn't walk away," he said with a heaviness to his voice. "I ran, didn't I?"

He looked on the small garden plot he'd scraped out of the forest floor many years ago. By rights he should have been knee deep in the compost as he readied the soil for this year's starters, but not this spring. Or the next. He ached too much to do little more than poke at the soil with his cane. He'd been around too long, he thought. Too many wild hunts. Too many people in the wrong place at the wrong time.

Like the three hikers more than twenty years ago. They made the mistake of traipsing around the same back country the creature had claimed for his own. All torn to pieces inside their tents. Their bodies: eaten by the wolf until it was full and then the other carrion feeders in the weeks after the attack. Their bones would never be discovered. He burned them in a pyre he'd constructed on a cold February night. He burned their belongings but kept their names to honor them.

They were always to be remembered. Even the nameless ones the monster tore apart as a much younger man's feral nature stalked the alleyways and side streets of the city. The crushing guilt. The self-loathing, knowing that all it would take to stop the beast would be his own bloodletting. He had always possessed the power to end his affliction, but he feared there would be no angel at the end of his walk through the light. Only darkness and the faces of the men, women, and children. All of them the monster butchered.

And too many aches the following morning when the fever subsided.

Over the years, the old man had taken to carving the names of streets into the trunks of trees so that he could find his way back to his cabin. His memory had its blank spots and the creature never found itself lost when the night was clear, and the frost had just set in. It reveled in its freedom in a hunt that could sometimes reach fifteen miles in one night. It oftentimes took the better part of the next day for the old man to find his way back home. Naked. Covered with blackfly and mosquito bites. Wintertime was the worst.

He remembered that first time entering the forest after abandoning his car when the gas finally ran out. A thousand and more fresh, wild scents filled his nostrils, not the stench of diesel from the city bus he would take to the edge of town. Far away from human beings.

Except the edge of town was never far enough as the beast would encounter human prey more often than not. He breathed in the forest deeply, hopefully sating the creature inside. The sounds of the forest were so different from that of the city, he felt foolish for thinking he might survive between moons. He had never built anything bigger than a table and chair before. Still, over his shoulder, a green duffle bag filled with tools to build a shelter and a rifle to hunt for food between the creature's feedings.

To find peace if such a thing existed at all.

The old man sat on the same scratch-covered rock shelf above the ravine he visited each time the moon was full and yellow as a cat's eye. It was here that he wished he might lose his balance mid-transformation and fall into the deep ravine below. If only fate would allow him a sin-free death. God knew the old man wasn't brave enough to throw himself off the ledge and kill the beast. God knew all things, didn't he? Even in the hearts of those cursed through no fault of their own. Eighty-one years, half of them in the woods. All that time spent hiding from the world of men and still they would find their way to him by chance or fate.

He remembered the rich American who'd paid a regal sum to hunt gray wolves and brown bears in the wilds. The old man's wilds. His creature's range. He remembered visiting the man's camp three days before a full moon to scare them off: the rich man and two other blustery types. He always showed them the old, jagged scar on his left neck and shoulder. A scar that looked like it came from a terrible bite. But no gray wolf or brown bear could leave a mark like the one on the old man's neck. A bear could knock a man's head off with one swipe of his paw. Gray wolves always ate what they killed and the thing that attacked him failed to kill him. He was lucky, he said.

He lied.

"In three nights will be a big moon," he'd told them. "The thing that attacked me is still out there. Your canvas tents won't save you. Guns won't either. You've been warned off now."

The trio of men shared a look and the American laughed so

hard he offered the strange man a place by the fire and a shot of whisky for his trouble. He'd never heard anything so ridiculous before and anyway, he'd taken down more than one bear if that's what the old man was on about.

"We're here for the week, bought and paid for," he said with all the authority of a man who believed his privilege included domain over the forest and the wild things. "We hunt every fall. There isn't a damned thing in the forest that we're afraid of because we're armed well and experienced hunters," the rich American said.

The old man had offered fair warning. It was in God's hands. Who knew? Perhaps they would shoot a bear between then and the full moon. He'd get his hide and leave. As for gray wolves, there hadn't been a sighting in many years. Something larger, more feral had moved into their range and claimed it for itself. He left the trio to their whisky and cigars and the rich American's boisterous laughter.

Three days came and went.

The old man visited the rock shelf just after suppertime, naked and shaking with fever. He never knew when precisely his blood would begin to boil. Sometimes the transformation took hold at moon's first light and other times the change wouldn't come until the silent hours. He'd awoken that morning remarkably pain-free, just as he did every morning before the change. His bent back straightened, his swollen, sore knees a memory.

All day long the old man's nostrils had filled with the scent of them. His cabin being directly downwind of the American's camp site a few miles northwest of the rock shelf. He could smell their shaving soap and their sweat. Their tobacco and their whisky. It was like giving directions to a buffet for a beast with an endless appetite.

He stood on the rock shelf and waited. The change finally took him near to midnight. An excruciating metamorphosis that always began with the old man being forced onto all fours as his human spine reconfigured itself. His sunken chest and rib cage cracked like tinder, growing in length and thickness. Enough space support the much larger organs. Its heart was three times the size of a human heart. It was the engine for the long hunt or the short take down of nearby prey.

The old man's mind burned with visions of the hunt. The human host's five senses were nothing compared to the information searing into his half-mad mind. The damp decomposition of the forest floor. The sounds of nearby deer resting in tall grass. The scent of human flesh.

Awash with feral sensations, bones snapped and then knitted back together as claws shaped like shark's teeth. Broken skin transformed into pads as coarse as sandpaper on the bottoms of the creature's feet. Haunches strained and twisted as the old man's toes stretched out of human proportion. Its rear claws dug into the rock beneath its feet leaving scratch marks as a grim reminder of the transformation. Silver hair sprouted across the creature's back growing thick with a black undercoat embedded in muscular flesh.

Its heartbeat was no longer human. Muscles and sinew rippled beneath a mane of newly grown silver fur. Powerful neck and jaw muscles formed as the old man's nose and upper jaw fused into a snout that could pick up the scent of prey in a blizzard. Human teeth fell out of its face replaced with shining white fangs that could crush a human's leg with a single bite. Old human eyes were replaced by blood-red orbs set deep beneath a rigid brow.

The fully transformed wolf sat on its haunches and panted like a dog in the blazing heat. Cool air brushed across its face and exposed chest offering some relief. It no longer needed to howl and announce its presence for there was nothing big enough and fierce enough in the forest to challenge it.

The wind picked up across the treetops and the wolf sniffed the air. Drool dripped from its teeth as its tongue lolled back and forth with each step. The hunt had begun, and the prey was nearby. The beast went off in a blur, kicking up large divots of forest turf under its feet. The bright round moon cast a blue-grey glow across the forest floor to where the men were camping. It knew there were three people. Each had its own distinct smell. With supernatural speed, the wolf climbed the steep incline leading up to the grassy plateau where there was always deer, moose, or elk or even a bear to take down and eat its fill. It could see the impression of the heat from their footprints in the ground.

But this was a different prey. One the creature hadn't tasted in an exceptionally long time. Its stomach rumbled loudly as it nimbly dashed through the forest. Smoke. Damp wood. More sweat.

It circled the trio of drunken men sitting around a comfortable looking campfire. They hadn't yet detected the wolf's presence; it wouldn't have mattered if they had. This night belonged to a monster.

It stepped out unhurriedly from the shadows. Then in a flash, it crashed into the first man, jaws ripping the victim's shoulder from its socket. Claws dug into flesh and the man's throat was gone next. Blood splashed onto the second man, the big talking man, as he fumbled with his rifle. The creature raised itself onto its hind legs and towered over him. It leaned in and ripped into his chest with snout, fangs, and claws. Then it started digging through the man's chest right into the ground beneath.

The screaming excited the wolf as it leaped onto the third man, his entrails spilled out like a bucket of chum. He dropped to his knees and the creature swiped at his neck, its claws slicing easily right down to the vertebrae. The man's head fell back as if on a hinge, held together by a flap of skin and a few pulsating tendons. A gusher of blood shot out of the man's neck and the wolf dug in to feed off its newfound prey. It blasted out a howl, an ungodly sound that echoed through the forest and deep into the night.

A good night for a werewolf. A bad night to be anywhere near the forest.

The old man and his memories. Alone on the rock shelf. The sharp crushing pain in the old man's chest. It hit like a freight train just as the transformation began. Half man and half wolf rolled onto its side, whining like a cub. It squirmed and bayed madly as it fell into the deep ravine. There were no angels at the end. How could there be? Even though God must be real because monsters lived and died under his gaze.

Hunting the Hunter

"Tracking and hunting are two different beasts. So, what are you going to use to destroy a werewolf if you ever manage to catch up? A man will always lose his life unless he understands that what he's hunting isn't just wild. It's explosively violent. Beyond feral. A werewolf is the ultimate hunter, and you have the audacity to think you'll be successful at killing one?

Listen now, you can't bring dogs for these kinds of hunts. Werewolves eat dogs and shit them out an hour and a half before dawn, see? And anyway, your dogs have probably caught wind of the creature and don't want any part of that day's hunt.

This here is northern Ontario. We've got woods here still blanketing most of the province, see? Snow up past your hips. We got predators and prey all over God's creation Tons of wildlife. You gotta know how to take down whatever is planning on eating you, natural or unnatural.

Looks like the world's biggest, meanest dog, right? I mean, its four feet tall at the shoulder if you can imagine such a thing. The wildest thing you'll lay eyes on in your life ... ever. But it's not a dog, so don't ever think that it can be bought off with a pound of ground chuck.

This monster is something filled with equal measure hunger and rage. It was human once. *Was* ... get it? You won't be reasoning with a werewolf. The minute you see it, kill it if you can. Now, should you wind up bitten or scratched by the beast and you survive, well, you're going to turn into one of those damned things next full moon.

I'm of a mind that the creature isn't evil. It's just hungry. But I'm not a northlands hick. I know that a human host could use that monster for evil purposes. That doesn't make the monster evil. It just means that you got to take that one down because its host likes to kill for pleasure.

I don't care to consider the ethics of hunting werewolves for sport but there has been some talk of rich people shelling out a pile of money to go after one of them cursed bastards. It's just not right. Those people are going to die in the most horrific manner your mind will allow, and they will have paid for the privilege."

Cold Moon at Midnight

Author's Note: the following is a letter from a human host to his fiancée. It is dated August 1906.

My Dearest, Bernadette:

This must be goodbye forever though I wish it were not so. An ancient evil has infected me. It has driven me to the edge of madness. Because of what I become when the moon is full, and the frost is on the land. Something unholy. It is because of the danger I pose that I am withdrawing from the world.

A cold moon at midnight is the only companion a cursed man like me can find and it wants its pounds of bleeding flesh. It's a madness, surely. One that makes me do the most terrible, awful things I dare not mention. I am past the Lord's gaze now and I do not have the courage to end my life. I am barely thirty-two. Such a monster lurks beneath my skin that it begs to come out even when there is no full moon. I know the doctors believe me to be insane and refuse to accept what they have seen; that I transform into the most fearsome of creatures when the full moon is high and bright.

They tried everything in their bags of tricks up to and including using electricity to shock the beast out of me. Patients and workers at the sanitarium were killed by the demon that has taken up residence inside me. I simply cannot control the creature because when the transformation is complete, I remember nothing. Perhaps that is best. Were I to remember, I don't know what I would do?

I have killed in the most terrible ways imaginable, and I will continue to do so every month under a full moon. I am leaving the country. Headed to a dangerous place that can accommodate one more dangerous creature. Australia with its wild outback and enormous crocodiles. Possibly even Tasmania.

My heart is broken. That mad dog. It was the largest animal I had ever seen. You know what attacked us that night was no woman. It was a predator of the highest order. And I am one of them. That terrible bite sealed my fate for all time. I thank God every day that I received the bite instead of you because it is a terrible thing to carry the knowledge that you are a doorway for the most ferocious of monsters for one night each month.

By the time you have received this, I will be on a steamship heading for the dangerous continent founded by criminals and thugs. It seems a fitting place for a man who transforms into a wolf, don't you think?

Always be safe on those full moon nights. I pray you will think of me fondly.

Farewell, William

Frozen to the Ground

"I have never seen a werewolf, but I believe they exist. As a forensic scientist, I am often called to examine victims for evidence. A bit of skin under their dead fingernails. A hair that doesn't belong to them. That kind of thing. When its murder, crime scenes are a horror show of some kind. Brain matter splattered on the wall above the cash register at the convenience store. A dumped body with a bullet hole in the back of the head. Killed execution style. You never get used to it but that's the working conditions.

There was one time we were called out to a crime scene during a cold snap with temperatures down to -20 Celsius. That goddamned wind, you can't escape it. The scene was a rural outdoor hockey rink near Ponoka. The victims were four late night players who were drunk as a skunk when they hit the ice as there were two empty liquor bottles on the player's bench.

They shouldn't have been out there in the first place on account of the cold. But, Jesus, something huge and hungry tore right through them. The ice along with the boards were splashed with gore that had been exposed to the sub-zero temperatures. All of it was frozen rock hard. And these huge animal prints, like a dog but as big as a bear. Frozen in the bloody slosh of the four dead hockey players, more prints

But the worst was yet to come.

We followed the trail in the snow by what I now honestly believe in my heart was a werewolf. We found one of the player's heads frozen to the ground. This was half a mile from the hockey rink. So, again I say, I have never seen a werewolf, but I sure do believe in them."

The Cattle Didn't Stand a Chance

"I've never seen a werewolf, but I did see something as big as a bear and faster than whale shit one time about a dozen years ago. Range cattle have a very exposed life at the best of times and there are always trespassers, but cattle do get out on their own. Sometimes you might see one on the side of the highway and you thank your lucky stars that it didn't wander out into traffic.

Sometimes you get wild animals taking down one or two cattle every few years. And then there was the time when I spotted some kind of huge-ass wolf except it couldn't be real because its size was beyond anything you'd ever see in the woods. I was a passenger heading into town for a night of drinking and general shit disturbing. Well, Jesus H. Christ, that monster slaughtered a dozen Charolais faster than the big abattoir in Brooks.

The cattle didn't stand a chance. Claws and teeth and superhuman speed. It wasn't even killing to feed itself because it didn't eat any of them poor Charolais. It just ripped them to pieces. No sir, something isn't right about an animal that can destroy a dozen prized cattle as quickly and easily as an industrial slaughterhouse. It was just wanton killing. A blood and shit splattered frozen dugout on a farm near Cremona.

Now I've seen all kinds of animals go after range cattle. I once saw a cougar attack a bull during a drought. I've seen wolves take down young cattle. They isolate the poor thing and then nip away at its haunches until it's too exhausted to continue running and too much blood has been lost. Then they'll feed. What I've seen left after a handful of wolves take down one of the herds, well, it sure as hell looks a lot like what I saw in that frozen dugout. But what the hell kind of monster can do that in no time at all? It went right through hundreds and hundreds of pounds of Grade A with ease.

But the thing I saw – well it was only for about thirty seconds as we drove past. It started to give chase and I told my partner Jimmy to goddamned floor it. We outran the beast but one image I will take with me to my grave is the sight of that monster standing on its two rear legs in the same manner as a human being who'd just lost a footrace. It was a wolf. Some kind of new breed maybe? Something that got contaminated by chemicals in a river or stream? I don't know but I did hear about a naked man being picked up by the Mounties at around dawn. He was just walking the highway headed toward Bragg Creek. Naked as the day he was born. Nope, I'll never forget that."

It Doesn't Hunt Like Anything I've Ever Encountered

"To date, nobody has been able to get into the mind of a werewolf, so we are left looking at the hunting habits of other fierce land-based predators for similarities. The creature is unnaturally fast. Speed is part of its hunting and attack arsenal. The fastest land mammal is the Cheetah. It can run faster than sixty miles an hour but only for short, powerful bursts. Speed is key for both creatures, but the werewolf also possesses supernatural endurance.

I was chased by a werewolf for two miles while driving my car home late one night. I know, it's just a dog that chases cars, right? I don't know of any land animal that can run at a constant clip of sixty miles an hour for two or three miles.

We know that it leaves huge footprints. Much larger than a gray wolf whose tracks are between three to five inches or so. The largest known wolf print found in Canada, is more than twice that size. They're heavy, too. Pushing through hard crusted snow on the Canadian prairie or thick mud in the Bay of Fundy, they leave a deep imprint. Weight estimates as high as five hundred and fifty pounds. Imagine carrying that immense weight and possessing the ability to run faster than sixty miles an hour.

Wolves, we know, are social creatures. Werewolves are not. The monster ... it doesn't hunt like anything I've ever encountered. It doesn't feed like any canine I've ever seen. The ferocity of its attack. It launches all that weight like a missile straight into its prey. Then it engages in a kind of butchery that simply doesn't exist in any land mammal save for homosapiens.

It digs into its prey with enormous claws and an intense savagery. It rips and tears and swallows flesh while scattering offal in all directions. It doesn't stay long when there is more prey nearby. It will attack anything breathing whose scent it catches. It won't stop. It will kill and kill and kill, all night long. All through the silent hours until the first streaks of pink and amber lift above the horizon. The ferocity. I can only compare it to that of sharks in the midst of a feeding frenzy.

Oh yes, the monsters are here. But let's not forget who the real apex predators are. It's us. Show me a canine, even a supernatural one ... show me a wild dog that can split an atom. Damned right we're the top of the food chain. Let's not ever forget that."

CHAPTER 3: SIMILAR ACCOUNTS, VARIOUS LOCATIONS

There are always witness accounts to a werewolf attack because there are moreof us (human beings) than there are of them (werewolves). In nearly every case, the witness speaks of the tremendous size of the creature. It looks like a wolf, but it doesn't. It's more feral, angrier looking.

A werewolf is hunger and rage taken monstrous form. The creature moves with supernatural speed. Victims don't even know they've been stalked by the time the creature moves in for the kill. An orgy of bloody violence will be the outcome.

It doesn't matter where or what time of night during the full moon. Does the lunar light bear some responsibility for creating such a murderous beast? Does the cold chill of a late winter night running up and down your spine really matter?

Wherever there are people there will also be werewolves. (And anything else that might want to eat people.)

These accounts only provide part of the picture but when compared to one another, there is not just similarity in attacks but the incredible violence. Victims died in terror while being eaten and torn apart.

A wild animal or a mad person is always to blame even though the witness each report seeing a four-legged predator of tremendous size. Long ears poking through a mane of dark fur. A long snout with enormous teeth. Huge paws. Claw marks like no other. The list goes on.

One wishes the beast dead after reading people's stories and hearing their voices. At the same time, you feel compassion for the human host whose life has been destroyed because they survived. A final thought: a werewolf carries no humanity in its makeup. It is a wild animal —the wildest on the planet. It doesn't matter where you are in the world, werewolves are the same. Brutal. Monstrous.

Terrifying.

I Saw It Kill from The Eighteenth Floor

"This would have been probably the mid-1980s or so. I was driving a tiny blue Honda Civic in those days. Just starting out in life. I rented an apartment with my then girlfriend on the eighteenth floor of the building. It was a bit pricey, but she was a nurse, and I was working as an X-Ray technician, so we were doing well financially. There was a balcony large enough for a lounger, a chair, a small table and of course our gas barbecue.

We had a view of the Bow River as it headed into downtown Calgary. Lots of bike paths and open spaces along the river. Autumn golden leaves as far as the eyes can see from all the poplar trees. It was just a special place, you know. Barbara, my girlfriend alerted me to an awful howling sound that I'd been doing my best to ignore as I watched Calgary take on Detroit.

It was cold, Christmas was in the air and Barbara dragged me onto the balcony because of an ungodly roaring sound. There was fresh snow that afternoon, about two or three inches. The full moon made the snow seem to sparkle and we spotted a man who was cross country skiing for his life it looked like, when the werewolf got him.

That's right, I said werewolf. I know what I saw. Barbara knew what she saw because she was there. I saw it kill from the eighteenth floor only a couple of weeks before Christmas.

At first, I thought it might be e bear which was entirely possible. The Bow flowed in from the mountains and there was nothing but bears and moose along the way. But this thing wasn't a bear. Not even close. Barbara, I remembered as I called the cops, said it looked like a giant wolverine. I think it looked like the biggest, meanest looking thing I'd ever seen Like something from the movies except more terrifying because it's eating you alive.

There was nothing we could do for the poor victim. I mean, if I had a rifle and a scope maybe I could have shot the thing dead, but I didn't. And the attack was over within three minutes.

The creature ripped the shit out of that poor bastard until his screams stopped. Then it moved on, tearing a piece of flesh from the man's chest.

Strangely, the creature turned so its back was to the horrific scene. Then it started kicking snow over the body with its powerful rear legs. Scarlet splashes frozen into the fresh snow. Torn fabric. It was just the worst thing I'd ever seen. Barbara and I broke up shortly after that."

Four Of My Six Screens Showed a Monster

"It's hard to talk about this because what I saw shouldn't be real. I had just graduated, and I got a job on a work site for a skyscraper. Only it was a big hole in the ground at the time as they were just getting started on the project. I worked along with the other security shifts, and we all got to know each other well. We worked in a big rental trailer. Six screens for six different sections of the job site. People were always breaking in and stealing copper, among other things. I was one of three women security staff.

I was working nights with my partner Dean and had just completed my first hour in a twelve-hour rotation. The bank of security screens were just to my left. To my right was a coffee maker and I poured myself a cup as something caught my eye on screen three. Even now, it's hard to believe what I was seeing but it was a man, naked, on his hands and knees. I grabbed the phone to call 911 because there wasn't enough money in security work to deal with a pervert who liked to get naked at industrial job sites.

"You seeing this?" I said to my partner. I remember he answered, something like "Oh man that's just gross." We sure changed our minds awful fast

I had the phone to the cops in one hand and a steaming cup of coffee in the other as the naked man started writhing on the ground like he was on fire. Only he started turning. I mean, he or it … well its arms and legs reformed into that of something canine. A high arched back with massive shoulders covered with fur that was growing out of the man's skin.

Even now a couple of years later, it just seems so unreal. We watched that poor man turn into a monster. It took about ten or so minutes and then the damned thing howled. Or roared. Somewhere between a howl and a roar. A sound you don't ever forget because nothing normal in the wild howled like that. It didn't sound like any kind of wolf howl from any Hinterland Who's-Who commercial.

It was a powerful, deep, rage-filled kind of shriek but low pitched, not high pitched at all. It sniffed the air then it starts prowling as we shut the goddamned light off in the trailer. We locked the doors too, but the monster must have known we were there. I'm sure it could smell the fear on us even from way down below in the pit.

My partner and I watched that creature prowl all over that job site. Four of my six screens showed a monster. Some angles better than others. One screen, nearest the facilities offered a head-on view.

Long ears like a wolf. A shaggy mane. Bigger than anything you've seen at the zoo. A thick, bushy tail of grey and white. Its eyes, deep set with big black pupils. Teeth. Jesus, the fucking teeth on it. Like ivory but razor-sharp like on what did they call them? Smilodon? Sabretooth Tiger or whatever?

The police were quick to arrive on the scene. That monster raced out of that hole and straight over the fence nearest the big Ford Explorer they were driving. Camera six showed the police had put the spotlight on the damned thing, and I think it just pissed the monster off.

It leaped onto the hood of the Explorer and punched the windshield in. Do you hear me? It fucking punched the windshield – now what animal knows how to do that? The glass shattered and it dove into the front seat of the car. Then ... BLAM! BLAM! BLAM! BLAM! BLAM!

We zoomed in and that's when the real horror show went into high gear. It tore into both cops and then fell over dead. All the fur, muscle, bulk, it just dissolved away and suddenly there's the naked guy from before. What in the actual fuck? Yeah, werewolves are real. Absolutely. Side note: all the CCTV from that night went missing."

The Thing Took Its Time Crossing

"I'm a railroad conductor. I sit across from the engineer. We work all hours every day of the year. Sometimes we take apart incoming trains, shuffle cars, and reassemble new trains. Sometimes we're on the road, it depends on what they call you up for but there's always work. It's a dangerous job.

You have to keep your wits about you when working for the railroad. A full train with two engines in the front and one in the middle can be heard for miles, but a kicked boxcar will roll up to you silently. If you don't have an eye for safety, you can count on being maimed or killed.

A werewolf? I don't know what the hell it was but there were some campers killed near to where we had just pulled into a siding. This was on the main subdivision in New Brunswick and if you've never been there, most of the province is beautiful forests. Lots of lakes and streams. Really friendly people. We were still about two hours outside of Moncton coming in from Edmundston. Something mean looking and big, covered with fur. It had a bloody part of the leg of a large deer or moose in its mouth. It stalked out of the bush maybe a hundred yards or so from the head end. (Of the train.)

The thing, and that's the only word to describe something that shouldn't exist, the thing took its time crossing. Of course, George, the engineer, put the big light on. Then we got a real good look at it because the damned thing stood up on its rear legs and sniffed the air. When you see something that is usually on four legs suddenly shift to two legs, well, that grabs a man's attention.

Bright yellow light cut through the darkness of the siding, reflecting off the top of the rails. You can see everything with that light on, nice and clear. It should have blinded the thing, but it didn't. It dropped back onto all fours and let go of the leg of venison. Then it came at us. Fast, Jesus was it fast. It was on the front of the engine in seconds.

I saw its face close up. A wolf's face but with a huge maw full of teeth. Eyes that cut through the brightness of a train engine's lamp. Claws that scraped and slashed away at the glass in front of me. Big goddamned claws, like three inches long and pointy as fuck. There was no fur on the claws, just bare skin. Pinkish looking.

There was no way the thing was getting through that glass. When the conductor shuts the door and locks it, nothing is getting in. Period. George gave the fucking thing a long blast of the horn and it did a vertical takeoff damned near. Landed square in front of us on the track and then it took off back into the bush.

Was it a werewolf? Well, it sure as hell wasn't any bear. It surely wasn't a gray wolf. I'd seen lots of them over the years. No, this thing was something else entirely. There was a full moon that night, I remember that."

Savage Battle Between Two Apex Predators

"Churchill Manitoba is a tiny speck of a town on Hudson's Bay. It's right on the water and for a large part of the year, that water is frozen. There is nearby boreal forest and there is also tundra. There is snow. There is cold and there are polar bears. The place is famous for them. You don't want to mess around when there are polar bears about as they are biggest thing on and off the ice in the north. I've lived here now (in Churchill) for about two years. I'm on a research grant from university studying the effects of climate change on boreal forests and artic flora

One-night last January, my partner and I were out on the land because the sky was on fire with emerald light flickering and dancing across the midnight sky. We wanted to get some shots of the sky because you never see a sky like that in the south. The moon was full and bright, and we could see the lights of the town of Churchill in the distance. Maybe two or three kilometers. Our Ford pickup never failed us the entire time I have been in the north, that night included. Of course, with bears everywhere we had a rifle in a rack behind us and Martin was an excellent shot.

We backed away from a scenic lookout; the northern lights giving the frozen water of the bay a curious blue-green hue. Martin was about to put the truck into drive when I stopped him. I told him to look out on the frozen shore – there was an exceptionally large male polar bear making its way in the direction of town.

There were always polar bears in town. People living in Churchill know how to deal with bears. Other things? Unnatural things? That's a completely different story.

Five and a half feet at the shoulder. Ten feet or more when a male polar bear rears up on its hind legs. If bears have excellent hearing and smell, they weren't working that night.

A wolf-thing was stalking the bear. Black fur set against a frozen white landscape, I call it a wolf-thing, because it looked like a wolf save for its enormous size. It wasn't as big as a male bear, but it was big enough to cause some damage before the bear killed it.

That would, of course, lead to a wounded bear roaming around the outskirts of Churchill. Not a good outcome for the bear or for anything that got in its way. A male polar bear. I don't care what anyone says, there are few things scarier than a pissed off polar bear and we were about to see one.

(*Author's note: I ask them how far away they were from the big fight.*)

How far away were they from our truck? A hundred meters or so.

The wolf-thing moved stealthily across the frozen shoreline, but a good sharp gust of arctic air must have blown the creature's scent the bear's way because it reared up to its full height just as the creature leaped, claws outstretched like a cat. Long ears and a thick shaggy mane and an unearthly roar. Primitive. Rage-filled.

The polar bear swiped its right forepaw at the creature, and it connected with the monster's head sending it tumbling into the snow. The bear then proceeded to repeatedly dive onto the wolf-thing with its front paws, the same way it catches a seal through an air hole. All that weight coming down and those huge teeth.

But the wolf-thing just took it. It started tearing at the bear's midsection with its rear claws as it bit into the bear's forepaw. The polar bear twisted its body and threw the wolf-thing off its right front leg. The creature landed in a roll a few feet away as the polar bear reared up again to its full height and roared right back at the monster.

But this was just the beginning of a titanic clash between the natural and unnatural. The wolf-thing quickly recovered and then raised itself up on its rear legs. The damned thing had to be about eight feet tall, and it started walking on its rear legs! It walked like a man would walk. Get it? Every scintilla of reason told me this was not possible. That what I was witnessing was an aberration.

Martin snapped me out of it.

"That's a fucking werewolf, Darlene," he whispered, his voice shaking. "And it's trying to take down a male polar bear. You should record this."

Video evidence was the last thing on my mind as the wolf-thing leaped onto the back of the bear and started digging at the poor bear's shoulders with its front claws. The bear managed to chomp onto the wolf thing's neck and suddenly it was the polar bear with the upper hand. I fumbled for my phone. I tapped the camera app and zoomed in. No fuzzy recordings like that one of Bigfoot walking through the bush looking at the camera.

They stood toe to toe, dark patches of blood on the bear's trunk, torn fur, and ripped tissue. The wolf-thing dove at the bear's neck, and he wasn't having any of that bullshit.

The bear bit into the wolf's neck and started shaking the monster. It rolled across the snow and went bipedal again. It dove over the bear's head, landing behind and then it pounced. It was on the bear's shoulders digging chunks of flesh and fur out of the mad creature.

That's when Martin grabbed the rifle and shot the monster. Then he shot the bear. Three rounds and it fell on its side and died. We drove closer to the scene and flashed the lights. There was a dead bear and a dead man on the ice on Hudson's Bay."

Howling Like Nothing Ever Heard

"We didn't see it, let's make that clear first off. You don't need to see something in order to believe it exists. I've never seen an atom, but I know that if you split one, you get a mushroom cloud. Our condo is new. We wanted to live downtown in our retirement. We were within walking distance of the central library. Arts, festivals, shops, galleries, you name it. Our place is eighteen floors up. Secure building. Underground parking. A security guard on site. Our corner balcony gives us one of the best views of the ocean. We entertain on occasion, but I'm getting beside the point.

There was a full moon, a harvest moon. A warm evening so we decided to sit on the balcony and look at that beautiful orange moon. We had just taken our seats on the lounge chairs when it happened. Howling like nothing ever heard. Everybody knows what a howling wolf sounds like or a dog, any dog.

Loud enough to be heard clearly over the busy streets below. It was announcing itself, anything that loud is going to be the meanest thing on four legs. I've heard the roar of grizzly bears; this was not a bear. This was not a wolf. It was something between the two species, I'll never know. That howling went on for a good fifteen minutes and then it stopped.

We read about the horrible killings that night, near our condominium. So, we didn't see it, we only heard it. Anybody in our building would have heard it.

Anybody within a ten-block radius would have heard it. Anybody within earshot at street level would have been a potential victim of ... whatever the hell it was. Werewolf. I keep going back to that. It was a werewolf."

It Was Partially Clad in A Torn Evening Gown

"You want to know what's happening in the city center? Where to avoid and where not to avoid? Where your presence might wind up getting you shot. You want to know what's happening, you talk to a street person. We see everything and nobody ever sees us, eh? Folks purposefully turn their eyes away. I'm not ashamed of being on the street. Sometimes life just sends you to the very bottom.

It was a wolf of some kind, but not a wolf, if that makes any sense. It was big enough to make me want to run like hell (which I did, looking over my shoulder every few seconds). It had me easy in the alley way behind the President Hotel. I ran, it stalked me. No clue why it didn't attack me.

It was fate that a large bouncer stepped outside into the alleyway for a smoke. That guy got it. I couldn't have saved the man because the creature's savagery was beyond anything I'd ever seen. It dug into that man's torso, tearing out huge chunks of flesh. It stood over the steaming corpse of the bouncer and howled with a sound that went right to your bowels.

And the goddamned thing, all fours, a bushy tail, and a face full of teeth that looked like they could shred just as well as its claws. But ... it was partially clad in a torn evening gown. Like it had been wearing it. No, I am not on any kind of medication. I know what I saw. That was a wolfwoman, no doubt in my mind.

I disappeared into an unlocked doorway – at a strip club if you can imagine. I hid out in a storage room and fell asleep. They woke me up and kicked me out a few hours later. There had been a killing in the alleyway. An awful killing, just brutal. I talked to the police, and they dismissed my account of what I saw. It was a wolfwoman, End of story."

A Goddamned Beast

"If I could draw you a picture of what I saw, it would be a scary looking stick figure monster. I couldn't get a shot of it with my phone. Up past North Bay. Nothing but forest and rocks. We built off the grid here. Not like crazy tinfoil hat type of off the grid, but more along the lines of saving the planet. We have solar panels on the cabin and outbuildings. Each building is self-sufficient in that regard.

We've got geo-thermal heating and cooling the house. There is beautiful view of the river valley, it explodes with colour each autumn, the valley.

It was the howling that caught our attention first off. Linda, our golden retriever, peed on the floor and that only happens when there is a bad thunderstorm. Then she ran off into the bedroom and hid underneath our bed. My wife, Connie, she joked that maybe it was a werewolf. I chuckled mildly at the suggestion that a man or woman could sprout fur and fangs each full moon and then go on a killing spree.

Emphasis on the killing spree part. Yes, there was a full moon when we heard that godawful howling. I remember looking up to see if there was a full moon, and of course, there was. There we were, my wife the dog and me under a full moon and something was howling in the distance. A big voice that sounded hungry as hell.

A downside to living off the grid is that you're on your own. You need a good four-wheel drive truck for when you truly need to go to town. We usually went to town once a month. Basic supplies with minimal packaging, if possible, that kind of thing. We had a pair of semi-automatic rifles and a shotgun. The sound of that thing. Must have been a goddamned monster because I've never heard an animal howl that way.

I walked out the door and onto the front step, keeping the door open behind me. Yellow-orange light spilled into the yard, cutting through the darkness. I flipped the spotlight on while Connie grabbed a rifle and handed it to me. She was already shouldering the shotgun. I did a scan of the property and didn't see anything. I was just about to go back in the house when there came the most awful roaring sound. Noise carries farther at night, so it was hard to pinpoint anything. Roaring overtop, a high-pitched shrieking that went on for about ten seconds and that was it. Silence.

The next day we went for a hike to investigate what we'd heard in the darkness only hours earlier. It took about twenty minutes before we found the bloodiest scene I've ever come across in the woods. I mean, you always see the occasional dead animal carcass partially consumed. Sometimes you encounter a skeleton of an elk laying in a bed of fur. Those are natural killings.

What we saw was unnatural. A dead moose cow lay across our path, the head was still attached, barely. There was offal scattered about, the furthest away was the moose's liver. About fifty feet from its remains which can only be described as pure gore.

You could see deep claw marks gouged into the dead animal's flesh. Its throat was ripped out. Lungs and heart were gone. Torn from inside the ribs that had been chewed and dug through. Blood everywhere and footprints that don't match anything Connie or I have ever seen.

Just these long claw marks. I've seen lots of bear prints as they have long claws. What we saw was nothing like that, end of story. Long claw marks dug deep into the forest floor. Footprints were huge; as wide as both of my hands side by side. We took pictures of the footprint and I kick myself now because we should have made a plaster cast of a few of them.

As I said, what we encountered was unnatural. Was it a werewolf? Wasn't it? Something tore apart an adult moose as easily as a kid tearing through wrapping paper on Christmas morning. We stay indoors on full moon nights, just in case."

It Was Huge Like the Harvest Moon

"Harvest moon is the most beautiful moon. Also, the most frightening because I will tell you right now that something huge like the harvest moon crossed the street in front of the donut shop where I worked the night shift. We all saw it, (the baker and two late-night customers) the werewolf. That's exactly what it was because it looked like a wolf only way bigger.

Like way, way bigger.

I mean it was a wolf, the size of a small car. No traffic on 28th Street at two in the morning except for enormous predators that look a hell of a lot like a mutant fucking wolf or something. The thing was half a block away from the store. We have a drive-thru window, and the building is effectively a glass box. If it wanted to come for us, we'd have been screwed. Instead, the thing finished crossing the road and headed into an open field and then into some farmland.

I recorded it for about twenty seconds on my phone until it disappeared into the low ground. They found a guy ripped to shit in a laneway about a mile from the store. Absolutely torn apart. It was a werewolf. Had to be."

We Shot the Evil SOB Dead

"My partner and I were responding to a noise complaint at an apartment complex when we encountered the first victim in the parking lot. It was the beginning of December. Christmas party season always kept us busy with domestics and drunk drivers and the occasional murder. The man's chest hand been torn open and there were big slash marks across this face. Dave, my partner, put the car in park.

He asked, 'What the hell kind of wild animal did that?'

I nodded quickly and said something like 'what if it isn't a wild animal?'

He took a moment and then opened the door and stepped out. "Normal procedure. Let's go."

Dave outranked me. If we came across a human perpetrator, then normal takedown procedure would apply. We always want to bring them in alive. Of course, if the perp came at either of us, we would fire on the assailant as per our training. We flashed our lights across the rest of the parking lot and then onto the remains.

There were bloody footprints in the snow. Big prints – like dog or wolf prints with deep gouges that were more like claw marks than nail marks. I remember thinking that we'd better call animal control for backup if the thing that made those footprints were an indication of its size.

We followed the footprints wherever they took us. About a minute passed before we saw the next victim. Between a couple of cars. He had just stepped out of his SUV because the dome light was still on, and the door was wide open. His mutilated remains lay about ten feet from the front of his vehicle. Torn clothing. I remember seeing how the stuffing from the man's winter coat was soaking up the blood and I nearly threw up. No shame in it. Dave puked. I said nothing.

Again, footprints in the blood and a trail to follow. I remember looking up and seeing the full moon. That's when a woman ran screaming from the entrance of the building. It pounced from out of nowhere and we'd have never seen it if the woman hadn't started screaming because of the snow.

The thing had white fur from head to tail. A head three times as large as a regular wolf. Fangs that looked like they belonged to something straight out of your worst nightmare. How big? Well, everyone knows how big an adult German Shepherd is. The thing that leaped out of nowhere at the lady was massive. Easily the size of a subcompact SUV. That woman would have been dead meat, but Dave and I emptied our personal weapons into the creature and the thing dropped like a heavy stone. When we went to check on the body the wolf was gone and instead there was a dead man who looked to be in his seventies. He still had a full head of hair, and it was as white as the snow. Just like the evil thing we shot dead.

The lady survived. The official report was the two killings were at the old man's hands. A very powerful old man, apparently. Our body cameras were confiscated. They confiscated the CCTV from the building. When the government doesn't want you to know, they will make sure you never find out. At any rate, we shot the evil SOB dead. The lady from the building left the province the last I'd heard."

CHAPTER 4: HUNTED

As we explore the latest restaurant delivery app on our smart phones, it's easy to forget how technology has made access to food a breeze for those with means. All you need is a valid credit card and a hand-held device. The world's food at your fingertips and then quickly, on your doorstep. With so much culinary variety at our disposal it's hard to believe that human beings might be a menu item for a predator, natural or supernatural.

We're supposed to be at the very top of the food chain so you can imagine the terror one must feel when they realize the huge dog circling them in the mostly empty parking garage at eleven at night isn't a dog at all. Or a bear. Or a mountain lion. It's a werewolf and it's about to attack. Sorry, but you're about to be eaten. There won't be time to say your prayers because you will be too busy screaming as the creature rips into your torso.

The following accounts are chilling, violent, awful. The creature is similar in each instance; from its method of stalking from the shadows to how it often circles prey just before it is about to attack. Be always aware when you're out on the night of a full moon. Better still, just stay home and you'll probably live to see tomorrow morning.

It Killed My Dog as She Tried to Protect Me

"The thing that attacked us ... (begins sobbing) ... Daisy was an American Staffordshire Terrier. Not afraid of a thing and always obedient. She picked up its scent early on, I realize now. She was becoming very unsettled on the leash. Her hackles were raised, I remember that.

The monster slithered out of a shadow about a hundred yards from me. It had wolf-like features, but distorted, twisted into a terrifying creature that was tall at the shoulder and had teeth like I've never seen on a canine before. It had short, powerful rear legs. A thin veil of fur over skin.

That sent me running. I could hear its paws beating against the pavement as the full moon's light made shadows look like they had come alive. I ran as fast as my legs could carry me. Then, I felt a warm rush of air on the back of my neck as the werewolf leaped over me, landing about five feet away. That's when Daisy broke her collar and attacked the creature. She dug her teeth into its left rear leg and the monster let out a howl I will take with me to my grave.

The werewolf reared up and managed to shake Daisy off its leg and my good girl attacked it for a second and final time. She leaped high enough to get her jaws clamped onto the monster's left forepaw. I nearly threw up when I saw a tattoo of a happy face just above its other forepaw. The werewolf howled in pain a second time as I ran for my life. Straight into traffic. I dodged and swerved to avoid getting run over.

Once I was on the other side of the street, I turned around to see the werewolf bite into my beautiful Daisy's muscular neck. It … (sobs) took her head off. The monster killed my dog as she tried to protect me. Daisy's sacrifice bought me some time to get across the busy boulevard.

The werewolf limped away, believe it or not. I hit 911 and nobody believed me. That's why you want a dog for protection that's brave and will sacrifice itself to save you. Get an American Staffordshire Terrier. My Daisy fought that thing and won, though she paid with her life. If there is a heaven, I know she's there waiting for me."

Three Dead at The Stadium

"The headline didn't tell the truth. Believe me, I was there and saw what happened. I ran for my fucking life, and I could hear its claws clicking against the shining cement floor across Mezzanine 6A. It wasn't just 'three dead at stadium,' it should have read 'Three Maintenance Staff Butchered' because that's what happened. Where was security? Well, they were just holed up inside their office on the other side of the stadium. Behind locked doors, it was later discovered. So, I was well and truly on my own.

I had just completed cleaning the men's washroom when I heard Danny screaming. Then Murray started screaming just as Danny's screams ended. Maybe five seconds. Both were all like, 'No, oh God no, please help me …' Just terrifying, man. I flew out of the men's washroom with the spare mop handle, like that was going to do anything useful at all against what I was looking at.

The biggest animal I'd seen with fur outside of a zoo. It was standing overtop of Murray whose chest looked torn open. Still clutching the stupid mop for dear life. I fumbled through my keys with my left hand, the creature roared or howled or something awful between the two sounds. Goes right to a man's bowels. I didn't have time to shit my pants as I stuck the gate key into the control box. The big metal cage rolled across the corridor, locking automatically on the other side.

And the monster started crashing into the cage wall. Throwing all its weight at it. I stood, dumbfounded for a few seconds as I got a really good look at the thing. It reared up on its back legs and leaned into the fence. Then it started tearing at the metal bars like it was trying to dig through. It started slashing at the fence with its front claws. It had a horrifying half-wolf, half-human face covered in blood. That's something I won't forget.

I turned and ran again, closing the next section of the stadium with my gate key. Called security on my radio. Shortest call ever, let me tell you. They saw what killed my co-workers. They started remotely closing sections of the stadium with the security cages. I ran down to field level and right through the home team tunnel. The gate closed automatically, and I was wondering if I would make out of this thing alive because it sure felt like the good people in security were locking me in with the goddamned monster.

My radio hissed and squawked loudly. Head of security came on. The guy had his shit together. Told all cleaning staff to get the hell out of the stadium. There were twenty other cleaners. Nineteen made it out of the stadium before its full lockdown.

They found the third body in the boiler room. His chest was torn open like the other two. Slash marks on the boiler. Deep, like a couple of inches. Everything went hush-hush about the boiler room and the slash marks.

They got the police special tactics team to set up firing positions on all exits and entry points. They set up a command post and linked into the security cameras. That's all I know as I was safely in my car and getting ready to race the hell away from the stadium and back to my apartment.

I know what I saw. I heard it kill two of my coworkers. I saw the aftermath. I ran for my life because I was next. Look, it was no more than ten feet away from me when it started smashing into the cage. I remember that it had to be eight feet tall standing up on its rear legs. It went bipedal and the last time I looked, all canines on the planet still used all four legs to get from here to there. This thing was a werewolf. This whole phenomenon of monsters happening all of a sudden.

I scoffed at first but after that last shift at the stadium, I believe in monsters. Even if the police eventually hauled a naked man covered in blood out in handcuffs just after dawn broke. Werewolves are real. All that shit is real. Nobody wants to believe it. Hell, I still don't want to believe it.

You know, there are social media channels devoted to this stuff. There are young people, all in their twenties and full of swagger, each devoted to shedding light on what happened at the stadium and other attacks worldwide.

I don't know what to think about the person who transforms into a monster. I don't know what the police did with the naked man they frog marched out of the stadium. But I heard there was an incident at the remand center a month later. More people died. The man from the stadium? Gone. Because he's a bloody werewolf and werewolves don't do Court of Queen's Bench."

I Tried to Run It Over

"Anybody who works the graveyard shift has a story or four to tell. I'm a heavy equipment operator for the city. It's a fancy way of saying that I drive a dump truck or steer a grader after the city gets hammered with a snowstorm. If you think pushing snow with heavy equipment at one in the morning is an easy job, it's not. Day or night, it takes skill to guide a grader down the street without burying a bus shelter in snow, or someone's car – because nobody pays attention to winter parking bans.

You always see wildlife entering the city limits when you're working overnight. Sometimes deer will wander onto the highway coming into town. Moose on the loose? Yeah, we've got those. Cougar sightings? Yep. Werewolf sightings? Oh, hell yes. I've seen one.

This would have been a few years back, that winter we had more snow than we knew what to do with. City blew the snow plowing budget in less than a month. People were using snowblowers to push the snow away from the foundations of their houses in advance of the spring melt.

I was tired as I'd been sitting behind the wheel of a dump truck heading to the city's north end. Two graders were ahead of me, and my job was to wait for the front-end loader to load me up with snow. Then I'd drive it off to one of the dumps the city has set aside for snow removal.

The loader had just filled the truck with my tenth load of the night when a huge animal began chasing the truck on the passenger side. It was unnaturally fast and within seconds it was on the bonnet of the truck. It started slashing at the windshield. It tore off the wipers and started pounding with both forepaws interlocked. Do you understand me?

The wolf thing just kept hammering away, determined to shatter the glass. I sped up and then jammed the air brakes to see if I could knock the fucking thing off. I was losing streetlight while this was going on. I let out a blast of the air horn. A long ... like thirty seconds blast, right? The monster went apeshit after that. It clamped its forepaws around each ear and slipped off the front of the truck. I gunned the engine, I tried to run it over, see?

It wasn't a bear. It wasn't a wild boar. We have a huge wild boar problem in the province. It had wolf-like features but the face of something straight out of hell. Understand? It stood in front of my truck, likely sizing up what to do next. I had three quarters of a tank of fuel and a reliable truck with a good air horn. If it tried for me again, I would blast it again and again and again. As much as it takes. Because what I saw that night isn't right. It's not normal.

I gunned the engine and went after the monster the best I could, hitting the air horn repeatedly. Whatever I did, it seemed to work because the monster headed across the field to my left and down into the river valley. It was a werewolf. I'd been hearing about this phenomenon of werewolves online and I initially thought it was crackpot BS. Not after that shift.

I saw a similar creature two more times, again at night. One attacked and I sent it on its merry way thanks to the air horn. The other one was about a month later, so February I think it was. Crossed my path on Circle Drive East from about a hundred meters in front of me.

Just crossed the road, no interest in me or my plow or my air horn. I carry a canned air horn in my lunch kit just in case. I think the monster's incredible hearing must just get the shit kicked out of it from a good long air horn blast."

You'll Know Terror When You Are Being Hunted

"Each fall, men and women take to the woods to hunt deer, moose, or bear. It's the annual event where people wearing bright fluorescent colours and who are armed to the teeth head to the woods for the big hunt. Surprised more of these people don't accidentally shoot each other every year. I was hunted one night while jogging around the Halifax Common. It's a patch of land right behind the Halifax Citadel.

I remember zipping by the empty skate park when I first heard the thing howling. My flat was just up off Robie Street near Quinpool Road. A kilometer to go until I got back to my place. Out of the corner of my eye I spotted a large dark-haired creature thundering down the forward slope of the hill behind the Citadel in my general direction. I swear to God, I have never seen any creature move like the thing tearing across the Commons with its mouth wide open. A mouth full of teeth that looked abnormally long and sharp. Like something I'd see on the savannah and not an urban park on the east coast of Canada. I started sprinting at this point.

I'm a skinny dude. There isn't much to me, but I am fast when I get a good head of steam. I ran for my goddamned life. Meanwhile, I could hear its paws thumping across the turf. I crossed Robie Street and ran into the lobby of a hotel. I started shouting to lock the doors to the building, that a wild animal was chasing me. I must have looked as scared as I felt because the front desk quickly had security not only lock the door, but they also guarded all the entrances.

And we saw it. Seven, eight of us saw the thing because it started to cross the street and then it ran back into the commons. Maybe the traffic even at that late hour was too much for the creature. Beats me.

You'll know terror when you're being hunted. When a wild animal is on your tail and you're next on the menu. I still run and I'm still a vegan, but I keep my exercise activities to daylight only.

I found out later about the two bodies found partly eaten inside the moat. That's a hell of a drop. Twenty or more feet. That creature managed to tear a couple of people apart in the moat and then somehow climb out of a very deep defensive trap. Then it must have caught my scent. We called the police and animal control. I don't think they got the damned thing. What kind of creature was it? A fucking werewolf. That's it, that's all. They're real and people better start to wake the hell up because these things are supernatural creatures.

I can't even get my head around that because the supernatural isn't supposed to exist. I have been reading online about the werewolf phenomenon all over the world.

There are supposedly thirty-five active werewolves in the world at the present time – based on reported werewolf attacks and found human remains. I don't know where any of this is leading us, but I know that I lucked out that night when the beast was on my ass. I totally lucked out. I should be dead."

Wrong Place at The Wrong Time

I was first to find the victims – well my Rottweiler was. We were out for our morning constitutional when Ajax picked up the scent. He dragged me across the highway and down the hill where we always run when heading to the beach. At first, I didn't want to believe what I was seeing. Right there on the beach.

They had a nice fire going from the looks of it and there were a good number of empty beer cans. A mild summer night on the beach with friends. Some drinks, some snacks, some music, and a warm fire. Straight up postcard moment save for the part where a big hairy monster ripped you and your friends apart.

I punched 911. Blood all over the sand. And of course, there were footprints of the canine variety, only much, much larger. I began taking pictures of the footprints with my smartphone. That's when a cop grabbed my shoulder and said, "Lady, we'll need that phone. I'll make sure you get it back."

Of course, I never got it back. I even called my city counselor to complain about the cops stealing my phone. Oh, the irony. Cops aren't supposed to steal ... unless there is a werewolf. Gotcha. (Author's note: she winks.)

As a matter of fact, city police have no record of ever having taken my phone from me. Hello cover-up. I wonder if they have a book for police and civic officials with instructions on how to manage impossible fantasy situations that should not exist in the real world. Like a werewolf, for example. No bear killed those beach party folks. There weren't any bear tracks.

The news said the prints are being referred to as canine prints of an unknown variety and unnaturally large size. I followed those tracks as far as I could, but the tide washed them away.

Wrong place at the wrong time, but Christ, what are people supposed to do? Stay indoors when there is a full moon? I've read online about how some people are hunting the things. That's basically insane in my books, but it wouldn't be the first-time human beings did something so obviously stupid it is worthy of ridicule."

Maybe Chainmail Might Save Your Bacon

"I used to be a skeptic, but there are too many reports now. I believe the damned things are real. They hunt and eat you. Key word: hunt. By the time you get to the eating part its already too late. People need to understand that when you go out during a full moon you're playing with fire.

Now I'm not saying lock yourself indoors. I mean, if you see a werewolf and you're out in your Chevy square body pickup, run the damned thing over. Put your truck in reverse and then run it over again. Keep running it over until the monster is dead because it's a killer. If it gets a chance to get at you through your windshield, it will smash through and then you're screwed.

I'm an entrepreneur. Me and my son. The werewolf phenomenon is not a conspiracy theory. There is more than enough physical evidence of the creature's existence after it kills. The world is filled with video cameras and people post evidence of the monsters on social media. (Muses: I wonder if Bigfoot is real since werewolves are real.)

Anyway, we know that Kevlar offers protection against the creatures but the cost of a Kevlar vest to protect your vital organs from werewolf attacks is prohibitive for most people. It shouldn't cost a small fortune for some protective gear if you go out on the night of a full moon. Chainmail might save your bacon, but it will weight you down against a creature that can already outrun the best athletes in the world. So, I see there is a market for lightweight, durable protective gear.

We know that werewolves have enhanced hearing. A gray wolf

can hear sounds over open ground that are ten miles away. Air horns work. An air horn with a minimal decibel rating of 150 should be part of a person's protective gear. If 150 decibels can harm human hearing, it stands to reason an air horn will send hearing sensitive animals scattering.

We have different sized horns available, and all meet that minimum 150 decibel rating. Obviously, we've never tried an air horn, but we've read and watched enough first-hand accounts of survivors who swore the air horn in the truck they were driving sent the monsters running for cover. That's proof enough.

We don't sell silver or bullets or silver bullets. Survival tools and air horns are part of a personal protective toolbox that everyone should utilize during a full moon. We're looking for investors as we would like to develop not just an affordable vest that can be worn as easily and as comfortably as an undershirt, but full body protective wear offering shoulder to foot protection against bites and slashes from the monster.

Obviously, physics can't be altered. If you're wearing protective gear, the creature might not be able to penetrate it to break flesh, but they can sure break bones and cause damage. At least you won't be torn to pieces.

Our approach is to provide clients with protective gear that will help them survive the first critical seconds of a werewolf attack. Enough time to use an air horn which we sell. We also sell aerosol wolf's bane. Wolves and dogs have an incredible sense of smell. A can of skunk spray and you might survive the attack. Bear spray should work as it's just aerosol cayenne pepper.

We have four different sizes of sprays with different spray distances. You see, I don't think anyone has really thought about protection when it comes to the phenomenon. Chances are you are not going to survive an attack without protective gear. The objective here is to ensure the monster steers the hell clear of you in the first place.

I can't speak to what happens if someone wears our gear and the werewolf manages to break the person's skin, though I doubt its possible with our protective gear.

It is the same metal material used in those Neptune shark suits. The wearer can survive a shark bite, they sure as hell must be able to survive a werewolf bite. A shark is king of the ocean predators. A werewolf is absolute master of land-based predators.

Author's note: I asked whether he and his son were trying to capitalize on fear. That's when he abruptly ended our online meeting.

Watch The Shadows at Night

"Me and another girl were just standing and waiting for the bus at around 11:30 one night. We had just come off my shifts at the big box store. Working retail is exhausting. We collapsed on the bus bench and then we shared a cigarette. From where we were standing the full moon cast long shadows. Streetlights on either side of the street, the shadows looking like two long rows of soldiers.

Except for one shadow that grabbed our attention because it was moving toward us. A couple of hundred yards away. Shaped like a huge dog. We thought it might be a bear and hightailed it across the parking lot and back into the store. Some things you just get a feeling about and the hairs on the back of my neck were standing at full attention. It started running at us, incredibly fast. I remember shining white teeth, and a murderous pair of eyes.

I was hysterical. I'll admit it. I've never been chased by anything before, so, naturally it had to be a werewolf, right? We lucked out because the thing had to cross the road and our bus ran it over. It didn't kill the thing, but it sure must have injured it. The beast limped away, back into the shadows, I guess.

Found out later they found a body torn apart about a mile from where I worked. In a parking lot. They are blaming it on a bear attack. The thing that came out of the shadows at us was not a bear. It wasn't a big dog or a mutant coyote.

It was a werewolf. A human turned into a monster on a full

moon. Just like in the movies except this thing doesn't strangle you to death. It eats you. Dark brown fur that went halfway down its back. A big muscular chest. Huge paws.

I'll always remember looking over my shoulder as that thing thundered up the road to get us. The sound of its paws crunching through the snow. Winter is King for werewolves when you think about it. Nights are way longer. More time to hunt.

I know what it feels like to be hunted, even if it was only for a few hundred yards. You'd be surprised how fast your legs will carry you when there is an enormous-fanged predator coming for you. Adrenaline rush or whatever, right?

Those shadows, you need to keep an eye on the ones that move because they'll get you every time of you don't."

Never Go into A Corn Maze on A Full Moon Night

"Autumn is my favorite time of the year. The air is crisp, trees are ablaze with colourful leaves of orange and red. And you do stupid things that put your life at risk because your boyfriend at the time is an idiot. Case in point: the corn maze out near Walden. My boyfriend James, his buddy Darrel, and his girlfriend Annie.

It's a full moon and of course our boyfriends decided that we absolutely MUST go through the corn maze. I didn't feel like going anywhere but home and I really should have kicked up more of a fuss.

Fine. I agreed to go provided they left the van's lights on so that I or Annie could be hoisted up above the corn to get our bearings if we got lost, which was entirely possible.

Darrel sparks up a joint and shares it with James. Annie and I pass because it's a chilly night, it's the middle of October and I just want to get this over with.

Yeah ... the howling was the first sign that we should have turned around and headed back to the van. Howling, roaring, sort of a mixture of the two. I looked up at the full moon and naturally you don't believe that a werewolf is the creature responsible for all the noise. Maybe a wolf, which should be more than enough reason for us to head back to the car, but nope.

Darrel wants to finish the maze and we've only just barely started it when the howling began. Annie and I dug our heels in so far as one can be firm with a couple of stoners who just want to get baked out of their minds and go through a corn maze. It didn't work. We didn't fight about it.

Annie and I headed back to the van which was parked on the shoulder. We were fifty feet away when the screaming started. They both screamed out to God to save them.

Annie and I dove into the van through the sliding doors and then we locked all the doors. I climbed behind the wheel and turned the key. I stepped on the gas and the rear tires spun madly, kicking up the loose gravel and sending it flying in all directions.

Then we saw it in the rear-view mirror. We saw it land on four legs right out of nowhere. Right out of the shadows. A werewolf and you could see that its face was covered with blood. There was nothing we could have done for Darrell or James.

I floored it, sending a spray of material at the monster, and giving me enough time to get back on the pavement. It started to give chase, but the big engine Darrell had just installed only a few weeks earlier provided more than enough power to put some distance between us and the creature.

We called the police. I kept on driving until I saw flashing red and blue lights. That's when I started flashing my headlights on and off to get the police cruiser's attention. He came to a stop as did we. I opened the driver's window and both Annie and I are just freaking out. Terrified. I can barely put a sentence together. Annie said, 'wolf … there was a wolf. It attacked our boyfriends in the corn maze.' Her voice was shaking the entire time.

The officer looked at his partner and said, "pull over to the side of the road. We'll go look." The pair drove away quickly, and I did as I was instructed, keeping the motor running the entire time. We watched through the rear windows above the bed as the police cruiser turned on the spotlight right down the middle of the highway.

Night turned into day under the power of the spotlight. The werewolf—it was fucking huge. In no time it was on the hood of the police cruiser. It started pounding at the windshield and tearing at the glass. There were gunshots. I don't know how many there were, just lots.

In the distance we spotted two more police cars headed our way, their red and blue lights flashing. Then we saw both officers get out of their car. They shot the thing a bunch of more times. There was a dead guy, naked. He was laying diagonally across the hood of their car. There were two more dead people in the corn maze, Darrel, and James. Both were attacked and killed by a wild man who was eventually shot and killed by the two officers.

It was a fucking werewolf. That shit is real. They covered it up. Do I miss Darrel? Yeah, I do. He deserved better than to go out that way. Same thing with James. So, never go into a corn maze on a full moon night. Just don't do it."

It Chased Me Through the Mall

"The mall has been here for forty years now. I remember going with my sister the day it opened for the first time – we were among the first one hundred or so. I had just turned fourteen. I work there as nighttime security all these years later. There are usually two people running indoor security for the mall at night. Or at least there was that night when a monster came for me. And, you know, when you first lay eyes on the werewolf, you're sort of glued to the ground.

I came to my senses and ran for my life. I radioed the other guard and got no answer. I was conducting a normal walkthrough when this happened, and he was doing an exterior patrol, so it was possible the radio was playing tricks. No answer, no answer. But I know this thing is on camera because we've got dozens of cameras all over the mall. Everything is recorded and stored on the cloud, right? Of course, our security booth is wide open in the middle of the mall so, it wasn't exactly offering any protection. I couldn't go back there.

It is surreal, being chased through a mall at one in the morning by a creature from your nightmares. Mostly because of the bad mall music that never shuts off. I ran for the north exit because my car was parked really close to the doors. If the thing was going to come for me, it would have to crash through the glass. Of course, I had to actually make it to my car alive. I shit you not, the thing jumped from the lower level to the main level. One moment it wasn't there and the next moment it was.

I just ran for my life, checking over my shoulder every few seconds. The thing was gaining on me and the only thing that saved me was the fact that it couldn't get a solid running grip on the waxed floor. I clump, clump, clumped all the way past the dry cleaner and the grocery store. Hitting the emergency exit handle and out the door.

My car is newer, and it automatically detects when I am close by. It unlocks the doors, so I don't have to fumble with my keys. Thank God for that. I dove into the car behind the wheel and slammed the door shut. I switched on the engine and turned on my dash cam because nobody was going to believe me.

The monster skidded to a stop in front of the doors. They are only automatic during operating hours, obviously. I caught about thirty seconds of footage which everybody knows about. Its online – Werewolf Trapped in Mall – I'm sure you've heard about it. I only put it out there after the police seized all the recordings from the mall cameras.

It chased me through the mall, but I had a good head start. My radio hisses and pops and there's a radio check from my partner. 'Get out of the building there's a wild animal up by the food floor!' He said he was already outside of the building. So, now what do you do when you have a werewolf trapped inside the mall? Nothing. The monster crashed through the glass door, injuring itself, I'm sure. And what kind of powerful creature was that. Those doors are solid. I floored it and radioed my partner to say put, and that I was coming in my car.

It's a big mall. Nearly half a million square feet of leasable space. The thing gave chase and I drove like my life depended on it because it did. The thing was gaining on me when another vehicle entered the parking lot from the street. The werewolf immediately leaped on the hood of that car and the driver started swerving, trying to knock it off. The creature slipped off once the driver jammed on the brakes and then … the most insane thing I have ever seen. The driver plowed that monster right into a cement barrier. Then he backed out and did it again. Then one more time for good measure.

The police were on their way and the werewolf, three times mashed into a cement barrier gets up slowly and the raises itself up on its rear legs. The thing healed itself, okay? I don't even know where to begin on how that could even be possible but then again, how could a werewolf be possible? I looked up at the night sky. Full moon. Crazy."

It Was Silent Until It Wasn't

"We're talking about something that shouldn't exist and I'm dead tired of debating it. People dig their heels in even though the evidence is clear, irrefutable, and right before their eyes. Mass denial instead of mass hysteria. There are lots of examples of people refusing to believe lots of things.

I counted as one of those non-believers until one of the monsters came at me. It was early, like 7:00 PM or so. Christmastime, the darkest time of the year. Well, the wife told me to go pick up a tree on the way home. It wasn't too cold or snowy, just light flurries, but we'd already received about a foot of the stuff since November.

I took the SUV out to the U-Pick just on the edge of town. There were five cars in the parking lot so, not really busy for a place only a few days before Christmas. I climbed out with Penny, our German Shepherd and headed over to the RV they were using for an office. I paid the man for a medium sized tree, and he handed me a saw, then pointed to a row of trees about a hundred feet away.

I dislike Christmas but crunching through the snow with my dog during a full moon got me feeling somewhat festive. I made a mental note to have a shot of rum in my eggnog when I got home to the wife and kids. Decorating the tree night was always a bit of a calamity at our house, the rum always helped fortify against not having fun. Penny was darting in and out of the first row of trees – they went about a hundred yards or so deep. Each one in review order as we used to say in the infantry.

I spotted a family fell a tree and begin dragging it to the parking lot. They were actually singing Christmas carols; it was that kind of special night. Except it would be remembered for the horror.

The U-Pick was a fifteen-minute drive in the country from our house on the south side. Lots of snow-covered farmland for miles in all directions. I was glad to be out with the dog. It wasn't too cold, minus ten or so. Saw in hand I trudged through the snow underneath the full moon.

Then I heard it, one godawful loud howl. The sound stopped me in my tracks. Stopped Penny, too. A second howl came, this time a bit louder than the first. Penny turned a ran faster than I'd ever seen her run in my life. We were just off the highway, and I gave chase as she headed to the parking lot and back to the car. I'd never seen her so scared, she stood next to the back hatch just shaking.

I decided to get in the car with Penny to calm her down and we'd try again in a few minutes. I pressed the unlock button on my key fob and opened the hatch. Penny dove into the back of the for dear life. I closed the hatch when I noticed six or seven people running like hell out of the U-Pick and straight to the parking lot. Running for their lives. Most of us will never encounter a person running for their life – be glad of it because if you see such things, you'd better start running yourself. I got behind the wheel and locked the doors as I started the car.

What could I do to help anyone? What could I do, I mean outside of calling the police which I did? The murderous creature went for the closest runner, a man with an axe in his hand, no less. As if that would do any good against a werewolf. I mean, maybe if you got a lucky shot in.

The victim fell face-first into the snow and the werewolf tore into his abdomen. Yes, it was a werewolf. It wasn't a bear, and it wasn't a wild person who is responsible for the gruesome deaths. They media is just reporting what the powers are telling them to report. It's too horrible to talk about because that man didn't have a chance. I don't think anybody has a chance against something that hunts from the darkness that way.

It was the most savage thing I had ever seen or heard. Pure rage from the creature. It roared while it did its grisly business. It dug and dug and ripped and tore through its victim. Blood splashing all over the packed snow of the parking lot. It was a werewolf, do you understand? It was a werewolf, and it was nothing like you saw in the movies. Huge. Rage. Hunger. All three rolled into one awful creature.

But Jesus, that monster. Big and hairy doesn't do any justice to the thing. Muscular and unnatural looking. A face like demon from a medieval woodcut. A long, partially hair-covered torso attached to a powerful pair of rear legs. Claws on its rear feet like talons; it kicked up large amounts of snow as it abandoned its first kill in favor on another terrified tree-buyer who just wasn't fast enough. I had the police on the line, and I got the hell out of there because that monster was going to kill anybody or any living thing that had the misfortune of crossing its path.

I have had occasion to question my mind after what I saw that night. It hunted in silence until it wasn't. A stealth predator which is different from wolves who hunt in packs and who don't use stealth. It had a tail, long and bushy. I remember that. It killed two more people including the owner of the U-Pick. Four people torn apart. Nothing I could have done to help them. Nothing I could have done."

Run For Your @#$% Life

"If you are being hunted by a werewolf, the odds are against your survival unless you are very lucky and, if you manage to keep your head about you. Run for your @#$% life is the best advice. Don't even second guess that weird feeling like you are being watched when you are out of doors and it's a full moon. Run. Run as fast as you can and get to safety.

That weird feeling you have exists as a result of evolution. Human evolution. It exists to make sure you don't get eaten whether you are Lucy the Australopithecus and it's 3.2 million years ago or now as a modern human. Follow your instincts. Just listen to them for a moment and it might save your life.

I was hunted once. Now I am the hunter for one night each month. I didn't listen to the inner voice that told me to stay home that night of the full moon when I survived a werewolf attack. I was out jogging along the river as I always did five nights a week.

I had run about three kilometers when I heard the godawful howling. Another three kilometers and I'd be back home, I thought. I hadn't made the connection between the howling and the fact that the werewolf phenomenon is real. Because 'all those' people were crackpots. Right up there with Yeti sightings and giants that still walk the Earth—or so I thought.

A man started screaming and begging for his life amid a terrifying roar. I kicked the afterburners in and began sprinting away from the river and back onto the sidewalk. I hadn't counted on the thump, thump, thump sound of my running shoes on the cold pavement. I looked over my shoulder and the thing was on my tail.

(Author's Note: I ask where the attack happened, and he said in Canmore. I suggested that it might have been a grizzly. An angry grizzly could outrun a thoroughbred racehorse in a sprint. He became very cross and let me have it. That ended the phone call.)

CHAPTER 5: FROM SILVER BULLETS TO WOLFSBANE

Wolfsbane or Monk's Hood is a poisonous plant. Deadly to humans and, according to tradition, if a werewolf makes any kind of contact with the flower it will burn the creature, weakening it. It's not true, obviously. The creature has enhanced healing. You'd need a lot of wolfsbane. Bullets are best when dealing with the creature, but that still requires a steady hand if you have any hope of hitting the monster. A shot in the head will kill it, assuming your ammunition is high-powered, and the werewolf is in range.

Most people are terrible shots and would no-doubt miss a head shot. Most people are having enough trouble believing what they're actually seeing as the monster readies itself to attack. Run or freeze in place. Either way, by now is too late.

Still, people are fighting back. Humans have a technological edge and are still the smartest hunters on the planet. We're just at that stage of human understanding where we are learning how to fight back. Fear is more deadly than the wolf, according to one account.

People Don't Take the Werewolf Phenomenon Seriously

"I worked for Canadian Intelligence and have recently retired. My husband worked for the Mounties. We sold the house and bought a motorhome as well as a piece of property in Arizona for winter. We wanted to see the country and that's exactly how we live now: as mobile as possible. During my time working for successive governments and four different mandate changes for our group, we knew the truth because there were boxes of files on the subject.

People don't take the werewolf phenomenon seriously. The first group that comes to mind are Deputy Ministers of the Crown. They need convincing and have seen a good share of the evidence thus far. They need convincing not of the proof of what they are seeing. No, they need convincing that they should look at the evidence free of the bureaucratic mindset that seems to cause things to grind to a halt whenever you are dealing with government.

And they do nothing about it. Their silence makes sense because we're in the cannot confirm or deny existence realm of security and intelligence. Were truth to be presented by a government department, even in sterile government-speak, the truth would be seen as official government policy.

You try to insulate your intelligence sources the best way that you can. Different names for different people but not the name they were born with. This was to protect those assets from being found out. Think werewolf witness protection except the person you are protecting is a werewolf for about eight to ten hours each month.

It's in the interests of national security that people continue not to take the werewolf problem seriously because government doesn't do pivoting on a subject terribly well. There are many educated people who are intelligence assets. There are universities studying the werewolf phenomenon, but you won't find them in the department of humanities or the faculty of law. Think agriculture.

That's all I am willing to say about how far the truth-hiding goes. I'm retired. My husband and I want to see the entire continent before we're swimming with werewolves (laughs). Anyway, that's more than I am prepared to say about the subject."

The Best Defense Is a Strong Offense

"Yes, I'm what you might call an amateur werewolf researcher. It's not a hobby. Horror movies relating to werewolves bug me. Nobody in werewolf films fights back and I'm here to tell your readers that there only hope is to fight back. We know what its weaknesses are: the dawn and exceptionally loud sounds like the horn on a transport truck. You need to remember that a werewolf hunts purely on instinct: it wants to eat. It wants to kill and continue eating until it has to leave and go back to wherever the hell werewolves go when they transform into a human being.

A dozen years ago I would have said to myself, "Scott, you're going to see a werewolf one day and it will change your life forever." I saw a werewolf as I was plowing snow for the Ministry of Highways one night. It was feeding on a fresh kill: a lone Hereford bull in a snow-covered field all by itself. A bull is a huge, muscular animal.

The creature I spotted in my headlights wasn't as big as a bull, but it was muscular at the shoulder. I kept pressing on as I had another sixty kilometers yet to plow. The thing didn't chase me, so maybe to the monster the plow looked like it was too big of a target to attack. Who knows? Anyway, that night changed everything.

The werewolf phenomenon was real. We need more evidence for science to find the truth of the damned things. Werewolves must be researched and yet they cannot be seriously researched because of tight control over the truth of the subject matter. Really, government is chasing its tail on this. No pun intended.

The truth will come out. I don't think we have long to wait.

(Author's Note: I ask him why he believes the truth will come out and his answer was straightforward and, in every way, true.)

We just don't know how long it will take for officials to admit the truth. But look at it this way: everyone has a smart phone, and each phone has a camera. A damned good camera compared to the Kodak Instamatic days. They have a link to social media. There are just far more cameras than there are werewolves.

If there are any government types reading this, give your heads a shake. These goddamned things plow right through anything that bleeds, don't you get it? You, me ...us? We're dog chow once every month unless we fight back.

The werewolf phenomenon is real, we still don't know much about the creatures, and we surely don't have anything resembling a head count.

Many researchers look to medieval history on how to protect against werewolves. Everything medieval was steeped in religious interpretation in those days. The thing is this: werewolves don't give a shit whether you're a catholic or a protestant so forget about a godly remedy. About the only medieval remedy worth mentioning is that of the manufacture of caltrops.

Surround your property with caltrops – I know of one man who made five hundred caltrops out of angle iron. I can't imagine how much work he put in but surely to hell we can produce the things on an industrial scale. and you have a chance of slowing the beast down enough for you to get a clean head shot with a minimum 5.56-millimetre ammunition. 7.62 millimeter is ideal, and you'll use less ammo.

A mixture of old technology and new. You could take one down with a bow but you're going to need a good number of arrows—one simply won't do the trick. Even if it is fired from a longbow. Forget about trick arrows; they only work in the movies.

Remember: werewolves have advanced healing. You have to hit hard, fast, and brutally if you're going to have a ghost of a chance of killing it.

It's recent news that werewolves can be sent running with a blast from of sound over 150 decibels. That makes perfect sense because the monsters have advanced hearing.

So far there have been know werewolf sprays developed but I defy anyone to tell me that pepper spray won't harm the creature. It's the next best thing to pouring acid into the monster's eyes. Once you've got the werewolf staggered you have a choice to make — flee or kill the thing.

If you're going to kill it, you need to make it bleed so much that its healing can't keep up. Drain the blood and slow it down. You need high volumes of ammunition fired quickly.

Empty your clip but make each shot count. Center of mass, every time. The best defense is a strong offense. Always remember that."

Thermal Imagery and Werewolves

"If a werewolf thinks it can use the cover of the night as part of its hunting arsenal, thermal imagery changes that equation considerably. It's not exactly a new technology; thermal imagery is often a platoon and section level tool that makes night operations that much more difficult for the average enemy soldier. I retired from the military a decade ago and thermal imagery is an exceptional tool for reconnaissance patrols as well as being vital if you are fighting in the defense. If something gives off a heat signature, thermal imagery will pick it up.

Werewolves are warm blooded. The creatures have a bright orange heat signature. My section encountered a werewolf during an exercise at Gagetown. Right there on the screen inside my carrier was the biggest four-legged heat signature I'd ever seen. And it was goddamned fast. It was hard to get a clearer picture as a result.

I don't know if this qualifies as fighting back but the werewolf dashed right up the middle of Range 16 quicker than anything I'd ever seen saver for a Cheetah. It was a night shoot. The full moon meant we didn't really have to worry too much about illumination.

The werewolf wasn't faster than a pair of .50 caliber machine guns ready to blow the damned thing to pieces. It wasn't faster than section level light machine guns either. I watched on my screen, each splash of blood a bright yellow dot. We cut it to ribbons.

We ceased fire and up went a couple of para-flares. A loud pop and then the night turns into day for about a minute or so as the flares float to the earth under their own parachute.

Of course, it wasn't a wolf when the green flag went up and we headed out to see what a monster looked like up closely. Just chunks of body parts all over the place. Human body parts. There were enormous wolf prints in the mud as it had rained heavy earlier that day. There were no human footprints, do you see?

Werewolves are as real as you are me. That's it. That's all."

Fight Back

"I can say in all humility that I didn't want to kill anything. I've never been violent in my life. I can't stand horror movies. But I killed one of those damned horrible things because it was going to kill me. Of course, it was a werewolf.

I was working late on an already late project that had to be completed by month's end, and I left the office around ten o'clock at night. I headed to the parkade, and no sooner had I stepped off the elevator when the howling nearly deafened me. It echoed, a horrible sound. Goes straight to your bowels.

I should have gone back indoors but I wanted to get home to my bed and my husband. I walked as quickly as possible to my SUV—I've got a SUV. I climbed in and locked the doors, then I pressed the start button. I put the car in reverse and quickly backed out, then I slipped into drive. The monster flew into the passenger door with the force of a wrecking ball. It climbed onto the running board on the passenger side. That's right. A four-legged wolf mutant thing became a two-legged wolf mutant thing. Hell yes, it was a werewolf.

It smashed a forepaw against the window, shattering it into millions of cubes. I knew that I'd be eaten alive in my SUV if I didn't do something, anything to save myself. What I learned that night is that to survive a werewolf attack, you have to fight back. Fight with all your might because your life depends on it.

I swerved the right side of the SUV against a cement pillar and scraped the monster off the side of my vehicle. It landed with a roll and then it launched itself against the back of the car. I slipped it into reverse and floored it. The SUV shot backwards and smashed into another cement pillar hard enough to send masonry falling to the ground in large chunks.

I put it in drive and moved ahead a few feet, then back to reverse and my SUV shot back, right into the creature's mid-section. I did it again and it threw up blood. I continued bashing the monster into the cement pillar until it slid down onto the pavement. I moved the car ahead into the 'get me the hell out of here position' and took a look back at the werewolf.

What I saw wasn't a werewolf anymore. It was half-human. Dissolving wolf-flesh revealed a pair of human legs. I quickly opened the driver's door and threw-up. The next time I looked at the thing that attacked me it was no longer a wolf. It was a man in his twenties or early thirties.

I put the SUV in park and quickly reviewed my front and rear dash cam recordings from the last two minutes. There it was: an enormous werewolf tumbling behind my SUV.

My rear camera caught that footage as well as the thing racing to the SUV and climbing on the back bumper. I got it downloaded onto my phone and then called 911. The police arrived within eight minutes and immediately went to work securing the area prior to the forensics people showing up.

I'd been shaken up. My mind officially blown. Werewolves were goddamned real, and I had been attacked by one. I fought back and killed the monster. I don't have any regrets that a young male was underneath all that werewolf flesh and I killed him. Except I didn't kill him, I killed a werewolf, and I had the proof.

No charges laid against me. The Crown didn't want to touch this with a twenty-foot pole. My dash cam was wiped clean when I got my SUV back. Anyway, you have to kill these things before they kill you. Werewolves might be a supernatural thing or maybe it's evolution or who knows, really? All I know is that they are real. I survived an attack. I killed one and lived to tell the tale. Obviously, I am part of the online movement to get the government to start telling the truth about the werewolf phenomenon."

They Don't Hunt in Packs

"They might look like a wolf, but they surely are something much more deadly. Savage attacks, lives and families destroyed, a monthly kill-fest for the creatures. That said, unlike actual wolves, they don't hunt in packs. Thank heaven for that because one werewolf can rip a man apart in seconds. A few seconds longer if its large livestock. Christ, if they hunted in packs, can you imagine the horror?

I am researching the werewolf phenomenon as part of my graduate studies. No, the university does not have a program about werewolves ... yet. There is a significant amount of physical evidence the authorities can no longer deny exists. The physical evidence that government agencies possess, I am told, goes to an incinerator. And what about the bodies of the people who turn into werewolves after the monster has been killed? Families claim them and if there is nobody they go into Potter's Field.

The knee-jerk reaction is to deny because government doesn't think the public can handle the truth. The trouble is that when the truth eventually does come out, the evidence comes from someone other than a government source. So, obfuscation kicks in. It's a serious process that governments use to cover these kinds of things up. And I have heard from a few sources that there are other kinds of arcane evidence that has been collected and hidden away. Evidence that has zero to do with werewolves and everything to do with other kinds of monsters.

This leaves me to believe that there might possibly be worse things out there than werewolves. I mean, of course human beings are the true apex predators. People just need to be reminded of that fact. Online courses exist to teach you how to survive a werewolf attack. They're free. Produced entirely on donations, they are of good quality. Each video teaches a different method of killing the monster.

It's vitally important to record any encounters with the beast. Unfortunately, until such a time as government is ready to accept the truth of werewolves in our midst, we must all of us take precautions. Again, thankfully these things aren't pack hunters. I suspect if a werewolf were to encounter another werewolf, there would be one epic battle. Maybe someone reading this has recorded such a titanic fight."

You Might Try to Poison Some Bait

"It's just another animal. Everyone needs to remember that because you must keep your head about you if you have any hope of surviving. Yes, it is supernaturally fast and savage, but human beings are still the smartest creature on the planet. I lead hunting parties of American hunters each fall in the north.

I'm not going to say what they are hunting for other than moose, deer, or bear. But, yes, you have a brain in your head so use your brain to kill the rotten thing.

You might try some poison bait. Grab a few pork tenderloins from the big warehouse store. Doctor them up and place them in the creature's known range. *(Author's note: I ask for clarification on how one would ascertain a werewolf's range.)*

It's a grim business but the only way to know the range of a werewolf is to keep track of the bodies whether human or animal. Werewolves have zero shits to give about what they eat during their monthly outing. You can leave the bait anywhere in that range, the big shaggy thing will smell it and will be on its way, licking its lips.

You know, there are accounts of werewolves dating back to Anglo Saxon times. Human beings managed to survive the monsters in a time of brutally hard living where the average life span was thirty-six. I've heard the Venerable Bede had written of such an encounter in the Ecclesiastical History of the English People, but the pages were removed.

Even back then everything had to be hidden away. Somewhere out there are the missing pages unless the Abbot of the Priory at the time decided to burn them. Either way, Bede made out okay and is a saint now, so good on him for trying to get the truth of these things recorded."

There Is No Magical Curse So Don't Look for Magical Answers

"I'm what you might call an amateur folklorist who deals specifically with the arcane. I study not just various mythologies relating to the werewolf and other unnatural phenomenon. *(Author's note: I ask what she means by unnatural phenomenon, and she just raised an eyebrow.)* I'm retired now from the public service. I've got time on my hands to really dig into the topic of werewolves and the best methods of ridding your village of the creature.

First off, there is no magical curse, so don't look for magical answers because magic in the sense that we understand magic to be is not real. It is an illusion. Sleight of hand. I try to think of the realm of magic as being proportionate to the level of human understanding. For example, if we had a time machine and could go back to what's commonly referred to as the dark ages and all we had was a disposable lighter, they would consider it to be magic. Similarly, if we were to be visited by aliens from another galaxy, we might consider their technology to be a form of magic as well. New medical discoveries are treated as a kind of magic. The list goes on, but the facts remain the same: hocus-pocus magic does not exist as a physical thing. Werewolves on the other hand very much do exist.

So, the reason that werewolves are steeped in mythology even now well into the new millennium, is because we have not studied the creatures. We have not studied those who have been attacked by a werewolf and survive. We really know nothing about the creatures other than they exist only for one night a month and anecdotal evidence but that's about it. Perhaps the creature is a master of the darkness—it must be as it only comes out at night.

There are no day walker werewolves and there is no war between werewolves and vampires to my knowledge and there is a lot more information out there about vampires than there is about werewolves. Both are killers, one just kills you without tearing your body apart and eating your organs. Of course, it's not like vampires are real or anything."

Locking The Human Hosts Away for One Night Each Month

"I'm an activist for various animal rights groups. Werewolves need to be protected as they are a rare species. Though the creatures are killers in every sense of the word, they are not thinking mammals in the way that human beings are. A werewolf only wants two things: to hunt and to feed.

It is driven purely by those two instincts. In this way, the creature is no different than any other land-based predator. The creature's host is not a monster. They are not lepers. They are not to be feared because of what they become when the moon is full. These people have rights. The same rights that you and I have. There has been no legislation put forward in any of the G-7 countries to deal with the rights of werewolves because they don't officially exist.

Government will have to be dragged kicking and screaming before they admit that werewolves are a thing. But no, they're not monsters, and they need to be protected. Locking them away for one night each month – that isn't too much to ask, is it? Everybody is safe.

Our official position is that werewolves are real, and they need to be protected from human beings. End of story."

We Hunt Them So You Don't Have To

"Ours is a group of concerned rural hunters. I once shot at an animal that did not resemble anything I'd ever seen before. It butchered my horses. I woke up, you see, they were screaming. Have you ever heard a horse scream? I missed my shot at the wolf by a mile, but my son shot it dead with ten rounds from his shotgun. That's how close the monster got to us. Jamie, my son said, "That's a werewolf, Dad. I thought it was all bullshit."

The entire pelt started falling off the creature in chunks; like it was being ripped off the host's body by a set of huge invisible claws. The fur, the muscle tissue, it all dissolved away to reveal the face of a man who had a Canada-wide warrant out for his arrest. Shot his brother and father. There were witnesses.

"I know, Jamie. I thought it was BS too." I said, nodding.

"You know, Dad," my son said as he checked the man's pulse. There was a big hole in its chest. "These werewolves could be anybody. Not just people with a warrant for their arrest."

Don't think I hadn't considered that possibility. What if the werewolf was just an accountant for the federal government? Or maybe a dentist. Who knows, right?

There were prints all-round the body leading up the forward slope of a field of sunflowers. Irony or what. My son recorded that thing on his head camera. He downloaded a copy of footage showing a great big wolf with unnaturally long fangs tearing out of the stable covered in blood. It spots us and the attack begins. You can see me shoot and miss.

Then the monster is in the air and Jamie blasts it with the shotgun. Blew the damned thing right out of the air. It landed hard on its back and my son continued blasting until the thing was dead. There's also footage of the transformation back. We've made that information available to the police who told the media the guy who was shot was a wanted man.

The government and the police realize that we're all doing a little dance right now, witnesses and the authorities. They know that we know the truth and that we know they know the truth but are lying to the public and to themselves. I'm for studying these creatures. How hard can it be to provide human hosts with a secure place for twelve hours each month. I'm not saying throw them in jail. But there should be a general acceptance that werewolves are quite real. They are here and they are hungry."

We Slay the Creatures

"There is no werewolf paradox if the werewolf is destroyed on consecrated ground, or by one of the blessed swords that we hunters carry as our primary weapon against the beasts. We are not warriors, but our faith in God and in our blessed swords gives us the courage to face the monsters head-on

We destroy the werewolf. Period. Often it is the werewolf who destroys a hunter. That goes with the territory, knowing that you might well be killed. Someone is going to die—either the monster or the one carrying a sword. We possess no magical powers. We slay the creatures. There is fear in my heart when I see that full moon cast its glow on empty streets because the best time to hunt is after midnight. During the silent hours you can always hear the monster. I follow the direction of the terrifying howling. It didn't take much time for the monster to turn its eyes my way.

We use the ground to our advantage. That's what we've trained for. Nobody should go into a forest or wooded area on the night of a full moon. The trees cast long shadows that twist and turn and blend into one another. The dark is darker in the woods so steer clear. Always. The same goes for unlit areas in town and country. An open field is the best piece of ground for a hunter. There are no shadows the werewolf can use to mask its presence. A high school parking lot. The varsity sports field. A soccer pitch. That is where I hunt, and the monsters typically come to me. I suspect it is all reflex with the werewolf. It catches my scent, and its hunger goes into high gear. Werewolves are guided by their stomach. Always remember that. No, the sword does not glow when werewolves are nearby.

As a priest. My duty is to hear the dying person's confession and to offer absolution. Most confess when they know they are moments away from ceasing to be. I think everybody suddenly becomes religious when they're about to pass."

CHAPTER 6: HOSTS

Hosts to the creature, it must be said, are also victims. Unless you are a human host yourself or you know of someone close to you who has been bitten and survived, you cannot imagine the weight these broken souls carry. You should count your blessings for that.

Those who realize what they are after that first transformation quickly end the curse by ending their lives, others still head for the wilds. The following are stories and accounts from hosts and those close to them.

Story: Pelly River Yukon and The Monster Inside

(From a personal journal dated September 1898. It was discovered inside a cave in Ross River Yukon in 1985.)

September 8, 1898.

Racing against the next full moon, it had taken all my money for the train to Edmonton. I sold father's pocket watch for rough transport overland to the place where the trails finally stopped, and the wilderness began. Father would miss the watch more than he would me.

I'd said little to the bald man with the wild mutton chops for the three-day trip riding shotgun on a horse cart. Not that he didn't attempt conversation.

"You're from the city. We get a couple of you each year. Off into the bush, never to be seen again. Maybe we hear from a trapper when they find human remains. The bush is wild for a reason. Don't think you haven't been warned, yeah?"

"The modern city kills far more people than the wilderness ever could," I sniffed, ending my silence. "This will do, actually." My driver shook his head as he tugged back on the reigns and brought the horses to a stop.

"You are a very serious young man ... stubborn. Well, it's your

funeral then and no bother to me. I guess this is as good a place as any for someone to disappear from all creation. Good luck to you, but don't think you haven't been warned."

That was nice. He tried to talk me out of venturing into the wilds of the northern forest and I nodded politely the entire time. I tipped my hat to the driver as I climbed off the cart and grabbed my duffle out of the back. I slipped my arms into its handles and wore it like a ruck sack.

"And to you, sir." I said, suddenly excited that what I had been planning for the last three cycles was finally coming to fruition. "Safe trip home."

He made a clicking sound and the horses plodded forward. He tipped his hat my way as he bounced and shook in the rickety old cart. "Beware of the wolves," he called out. "No doubt already caught a whiff of you, me and the horses by now. At least I've got my pistol and a shotgun."

"Thank you again," I said, offering a little bow. He snapped the reigns and made another clicking sound. I watched as the horse cart disappeared around a bend in the trail.

We had followed the Pelly River for about twenty miles before I decided I was far enough from humanity that I wouldn't harm a soul when the transformation occurred. I would become a man of the land, just like any pioneer or explorer. And perhaps the predators in the area might catch a whiff of the thing living underneath my skin. They might steer clear of me. I am unaware if I can change into the creature outside of a full moon. It might come in handy if I were to wind up cornered by an angry grizzly.

I have only transformed into the monster three times. After the debacle of the first change, I made efforts to ensure that I was clear of innocents. I was an innocent once. A werewolf took a piece out of my leg, and I walk with a limp now.

I change into a terrifying beast if the thing that bit me was any indication. Taller than a man at the shoulder and fast as the devil. To date, the monster inside has killed twice: a pair of prowlers. Their mangled remains were found in front of a locked carriage house. Mixed in with the blood and gore were lock picking tools and a small handgun.

I have slaughtered far too many sheep for anyone's good. I have seen the poor dead creatures the morning after the second change. I awoke naked and cold and covered with blood. All around me were the shredded corpses of fifteen sheep. Heads torn off. Throats ripped out. Each one, disemboweled.

The pain of the transformation is beyond words. There is no equivalent to the torture of having your entire physiology reformed in a matter of fifteen or twenty minutes. The monster inside doesn't know it is a monster. It just knows that it must feed. Its hunger is a force that drives it.

From the time I hopped off the horse cart to the next full moon was three nights. With a compass keeping me on a northwest bearing, I marched for two days through pristine forest no man had ever set foot in. The Yukon is the most magical place – the golden leaves in the autumn. The crisp air and the late autumn sun hanging low in the sky. The blinding snow that can kill a man as easily as any woodland predator.

On the third day, I decided I was far enough away to set up a small campsite. I built a lean-to out of pine boughs and found more than enough dried wood to keep a fire going round the clock.

That third night the full moon cleared the mountain range and shone down into the little clearing where I'd built my camp. I knew enough to take my clothes off rather than have the beast destroy them by tearing them to shreds. The fever took me as silver-blue moonlight poured itself over the face of the forest.

So much damned pain. Blood so hot it feels that your veins are going to burn up. The hunger. Dear God, it is all-consuming. It's as if you have been kept locked away and forcibly starved for weeks. Dreams of warm blood splashing out of prey. Then rage. Pure, unfiltered anger. Hatred of the day. Loathing the sun and the morning.

Then you double over as your skeleton cracks and breaks and then reassembles into a frame that bears no resemblance to the human being's skeleton. Then nothing. No memory. Just morning light in your eyes. A sick stomach and blood smeared face. What have I done? What have I done? Of course, I am off to the wilds because I cannot allow the monster to murder another person. I must remain in the peace and tranquility of the forest.

Not Every Soul Is Damned in The Same Way

"I've spent a career solving murders. Thirty years, I've lost count of the number of investigations I was involved with. Most of the time we caught the murderer and brought the son of a bitch in alive. That means you unfortunately wind up getting up close and personal with killers. And you don't want to, but sometimes you pause and consider that once upon a time, they hadn't taken the wrong path in life.

Before they killed someone, they still had a perfectly good soul. I think we all are born with perfectly good souls. It's just what we do in life that can damn a man to misery right up until the end. After that ... who knows?

There was one case I worked, this would have been about 1993 or so. Three mutilated bodies ... each was partially eaten. Now if the crime scene had been in the woods, you might explain things by the fact that there are a hell of a lot of carrion eaters in the woods. But this crime scene was the loading bay of a department store.

Three nighttime staff waiting for the arrival of a truckload of goods. Poor bastard driving the truck was first on the scene.

What kind of predator partially consumes a human victim in the middle of the goddamned city? What is the name of that beast? How can such ferocity live inside something that the Lord created?

When we reviewed the CCTV from the loading bay what we saw was something unnatural. Like nothing I'd ever seen. You'd think it was a dog at first glance. But then you zoom in and look closer and that thing is some kind of wolf-hybrid. Terrifying.

Maybe it escaped from a lab or something? But the size of the thing, easily the size of a small car. We slowed down the footage, the wolf-thing went through them like a locomotive with goddamned teeth and claws. Fast … unnaturally fast. It just appeared out of a small alleyway leading to another loading dock.

It tore those poor bastards apart. Bloodiest thing I have ever seen on the job. To date, it's unsolved. The CCTV footage disappeared somehow. This seems to happen a lot when there is footage. I wonder what the powers that be do with all of that stuff.

Over the years, I've read about similar attacks in countries all over the world. Victims found partially eaten, their bodies destroyed. Huge footprints, end of story. But the thing about the one back in 1993, that first monster. That creature still had a torn shirt hanging from its neck and chest.

Now you explain what kind of soul is damned to that kind of existence. Not every soul is damned in the same way and from what I've read about the creatures, it's victims who survive that become monsters. It wasn't their fault they were bitten.

So … what are they supposed to do? The good book says you're damned for all eternity if you off yourself. Between changes, well you just know the poor bastard is torturing himself wanting to die because no man wants to kill unless he is forced to. And even then, most people just don't have the killer's soul. Cold and self-aggrandizing. Sociopathic.

I know one thing: I'd like to introduce some of the murderers I'd put away to whatever the hell that creature was that killed those poor workers back in '93."

Locked Away Each Month

"Well, I married her not knowing that she was what she was. Margaret, she left home in '43 and became a nurse. Soon enough she was in England getting everything ready for the field hospitals that would be needed during Operation Overlord. That's right, my sweetie was in on the invasion of Europe. (I was back home working the farm as an essential worker.

I tried to join up – the artillery – they wouldn't take me. Said I was too short and too sickly looking.) She was overseas right up until November 1945 when she disembarked at Halifax. We took the train out west. Got married on the train, can you believe that they did things like that once upon a time?

I saw the scar on her left shoulder. A traumatic wound, about eight inches in length and all jagged. Like something took a bite out of her which, it turns out, she said happened to her only six months earlier while on leave in London. Nearly died

A wolf, she told me, had attacked her while she was waiting at a bus stop near the docks. It attacked and killed two men waiting for the same bus before it turned on Margaret. Got a bite into her shoulder. Next thing she remembers is waking up in hospital. Newspapers talked of a gruesome killing down by the docks and that was it.

But she changed, of course. While still in London. I don't know who she attacked or whether they might have lived or died. Now when I hear all of this the first time, it's unbelievable. But you know, when the person you love and who loves you back is telling you the God's truth, you can see it in their eyes. I chose to believe Margaret in spite of the unbelievable circumstances that she described while overseas.

Our train pulled into Winnipeg at 11 AM and we were on our way to the farm out near Brandon by 11:30 AM. When we got home, she was more than pleased with the place I'd made for her. It used to be an Eaton's house. I did a few alterations and turned it into something you could maybe even raise a family in.

Of course, that was never to be. Children.

Once we got home Margaret told me build a room that where she could be locked away for the full moon. I didn't exactly know what wolf-proof might be, but I figured a steel cage made from rebar might do the trick. That would take time to build, and a full moon was only ten days away.

Inside the barn is where I built the safe room where she would be locked away for twelve hours each month. I dug a square pit about twelve feet wide and twelve feet deep. Then I bricked in the walls of the pit.

It was a brick box in the ground in the middle of a barn. I covered the pit with corrugated steel reinforced by angle iron. On top of that, I would park the tractor and the grain truck. In Margaret went that first night. She told me to stay with her and to shoot her in the head if the wolf managed to crawl out of its prison. It never did get out.

The things we do for love. Margaret loved me with all her heart, and I loved her back. Part of me thought she might have been shell shocked while overseas, but that first night cleared up any misunderstandings that might have existed on my part. Her screams from fifteen feet below in a bricked-up room were enough to bring tears to my eyes.

Only when the sun was above the horizon was I to move the tractor and truck and lift the metal cover off the box in the ground. But I did see through a crack in the metal. The biggest wolf I'd ever seen. Pacing back and forth.

The brickwork I'd installed was covered with bloody scratches. Margaret's dress was ripped to shreds. Its muscles rippled through its shining fur. It looked up at me once, glowing red eyes. Like a pair of shiny rubies. It bared its teeth: long, sharp, and deadly.

It shouldn't have been real, yet there it was. My sweet Margaret. Bitten by the same thing that was pacing the floor of a homemade cell I'd built with my own hands. We kept it a secret all those years we were together. Until that day when I lost my poor Margaret to a drunk driver in '67."

Doing The Devil's Work

"My father was a good man. He worked all hours to put food on the table. It was just Dad, Mum, me, and my little brother Warren. We had a little house down by the refinery. The air smelled sour and oily at all hours of the day. But Dad was a company man. Did what they told him. Made his way into a foreman's role. Only problem was he got stuck on the night shift. The thing that killed him was doing the Devil's work that night.

My poor father was killed while driving a company pickup truck near the southwest corner of the refinery. Nearest the straights. Killed inside the truck. Mutilated beyond recognition. And the man who was in the passenger seat? He disappeared off the face of the Earth.

Police couldn't explain how a man could wind up butchered inside the cab of a pickup truck. The interior, aside from being covered with gore was also torn to ribbons. The seat was shredded and there were dreadful nail marks dug into the dashboard. The radio was playing George Jones when they found him."

The Man Who Said He Was Damned

"This would have been just before the dot com bubble burst, so, 1999 or thereabout. I was employed as a systems analyst, working my butt off! Everyone was afraid of the big Y2K bug and companies were poaching analysts from each other for a lot of money. I did well those years. I lived off Jarvis near St. Lawrence Market and if you've never been, you need to go. I was working to make as much money as I could in those days because everyone knew that it couldn't last forever. The work, I mean.

I didn't own a car because I lived in downtown Toronto. I took the train everywhere, mostly. I tried riding a bicycle a few times but the drivers in Canada's largest city were huge assholes toward cyclists. I didn't feel like risking my life for a damned bike. I walked a lot in those days. Never took a taxi in downtown Toronto, except for the one time which I'll share with you now.

It was shortly after 6:00 PM. Late September. I'd worked a couple of extra hours because time and a half was easy money to earn. Just do an hour or two extra each week and watch your paycheque grow. I needed a few things, so, I stopped off at the market. Then I hailed a cab because as luck would have it, I broke my right heel on a sidewalk grate. Four blocks to my apartment and me with only one good shoe. (Since then, I wear sneakers to work.).

The driver, a blonde-haired man of about thirty or so and exceptionally polite. He kept calling me *ma'am*. Clean shaven. Anyway, he didn't charge me for the fare which was only about eight dollars or so. I gave him a twenty for being generous.

"You're my last ever fare," he said, quickly glancing down at the twenty and then over to his Timex. "And the moon will be rising soon. Stay indoors because tonight a damned soul will turn into a monster. Don't bother calling the cops about it, they won't listen. They never do. I try each month"

I knew a kook when I saw one. You get lots of kooks when you work downtown.

"A monster?" I asked, innocently. A bad move. I should have politely nodded my head and then backed into my building, but I was fumbling with my purse, looking desperately for my security card that would get the door open.

"You know how it is, ma'am," he said sounding polite and business-like for a kook. "Bad things happen to good people. It's always the way it goes and you're good people. You stay indoors now."

He climbed into the taxi and pulled away into traffic. I hobbled backward to the door and flashed my entrance card. The door buzzed and seconds later I was in the carpeted foyer. I removed my shoes and tossed them in a trash can near the elevator. My apartment was on the eighth floor. It had a balcony that could barely sit two people on plastic lawn chairs. I had paid far too much when I bought the apartment, but my real estate agent kept telling me that his crystal ball said that Toronto and Vancouver will have the most expensive housing in the world. He wasn't wrong about that. I kept the apartment, renting it out. I cleaned up when I sold it a few years back.

wThat taxi driver. They found his shirtless body in the cab underneath the Gardner Expressway. Poor man killed himself – pumped in carbon monoxide. The real story was the condition of the taxi, I mean, the interior. It had been ripped apart. All vinyl and stuffing everywhere. Scratches all over the dashboard and the headliner. Huge gashes. Like something with enormous claws. The dead man hadn't a scratch on him, but the papers said he was sporting a large scar on his right forearm. Like something took a bite out of him.

The man who said he was damned was dead by his own hand. There was never any investigation into what tore apart the interior of the man's taxicab and the car was sent to the crusher. What else might have been in the car, eh?. I'll never know but one thing I can say is the dead man had my twenty dollars in the pocket of his torn jeans when they pulled him out.

It's a sad story. I think the poor man was doomed. I've met people like that. There's nothing that can be done for them because fate always finds a way to put a target on their backs. And the churches talk about a loving god. Who mourned for the taxi driver? I did. I still do all these years later."

Some Things Are Beyond Science

"There are limitations to the scientific method. A rigorous process, it's the best we have at the current time. Maybe that will change one day when artificial intelligence is running the world. It's already happening. Human beings are a relatively new species when intelligence and self-awareness are the markers of independent thought. Thinking about tomorrow. Planning for the future. That kind of thing. We've only been around for about two hundred thousand years. That's honestly a fart in the breeze of a cosmic sky. Blink! We're here. Blink! We've been extinct for a millennium.

You're asking me if werewolves exist and every scientific molecule in my body is shrieking NO, NO, NO! There's no such things as werewolves. Even though part of me wonders if we're talking about another branch of evolution. How many creatures already exist which change under the light of a full moon? Surely none if you are talking about turning from one species into another.

That doesn't entirely work with our understanding of evolution. And yet there are scores of unsolved deaths around the world. Each one sharing a similar trait: death by extreme violence and partially eaten remains. Every year authorities find human remains that have been so violated that saying the victims were mutilated would be a compliment. Experts from the universities are called in. There is no natural creature that kills in such a fashion.

This must be the work of a madman. Call in the psychiatrist. I mean, who knows, right? Let's face it. If werewolves are a thing, then what the hell else is out there? And while we're at it, let's identify the ones that see human beings as food. Some things are beyond science. Werewolves are usually associated with Bigfoot and UFO's. Grist for the scandal sheets at the supermarket checkout.

Unless someone successfully captures one of these creatures and it can be studied, etc.

The moon is the catalyst for a man to change into a wolf. Historically these men were believed to be delusional. It's only since the introduction of photography that we are able to stitch together a profile of the monsters.

If they are real, that is. Now that every smart phone on the planet has a super camera, it's now that we're seeing more and more evidence of a physiological phenomenon.

That's what we're calling it in my circles. Werewolves are a physiological phenomenon. It just so happens to eat people."

The Werewolf Paradox

"The term 'host' only came into use in the last few years. Before that, people like me were just cursed. There was always some kind of bullshit religious element to it. So, you've heard of the werewolf paradox, right? The one that says I need to kill myself, but if I kill myself, I go straight to Hell. So, I can't kill myself. Also, they won't bury me in consecrated ground. See? There's the paradox. You're screwed if you live, and you're screwed if you die.

Like I said there is always a religious element to this. The house is stacked against you just like in Vegas. It was in Vegas that I was attacked by the thing that I now transform into. In hindsight, of course Las Vegas had and may continue to have a resident werewolf. It makes perfect sense, really.

The good book says to love thy neighbor. It doesn't say eat thy neighbor each full moon. So, you can imagine, relationships are impossible. Procreation? It's all about the werewolf's bloodline so, no werewolf babies please.

I had a boyfriend. He slapped me around once. Something ate him. I occupy two worlds now. I'm beyond giving a shit at this point."

Searching For the First Werewolf

"I get paid to think great thoughts. As head of the philosophy department, I am always looking for questions in need of answers as they relate to the human condition. The facts are there for any and all to see nowadays thanks to technology. A human being transforms into a fearsome monster that may or may not resemble a wolf. Video evidence. Digital evidence. It's all online. And somewhere out there, someone must have been the first person to transform. What's happening, I believe, is an evolutionary event. Within all living things. Something had to be the first one.

How far back in history does that search take you? Where do you look? Nobody believes in werewolves. I know that I shouldn't believe in them either and yet, I must believe in them if I look critically at the evidence. Having viewed hundreds of crime scene photographs with similar victimology. Bodies torn to bits. Partially eaten. Ragged wounds across face, neck, and chest. Substantial amounts of flesh and muscle tissue just gone.

There had to be a first one. But this is where science and folklore clash. Much of the scientific establishment refuses to believe in the phenomenon. I mean, it's not like there's an annual conference on the werewolf phenomenon with sponsorship from big pharma. It's not like we've sequenced the werewolf genome.

And another question: does the werewolf exist when in human form? It has to go somewhere, doesn't it? It exists and yet it does not. It is real and a threat and then it disappears for another month. How can something be and not be at the same time?

There has been an increase in killings underneath a full moon. Separate of the human-on-human killings which happen every day, of course. I feel for those families whose loved ones have been the victim of a werewolf. I wish there were answers but in order to find them we must first accept what our eyes can now see, and our ears can now hear."

I Want to Live

(Author's Note: A police investigation of a dead suspect's small home in northern Quebec turned up a journal of the man's last few years. It is a surprisingly honest account, and the author does not regret that he is a host to the monster.)

"I didn't ask to become what I am. It's funny, I don't even know what I look like when the transformation ends, and the wolf has come back into the human world. Yet, I know what I've done because I've read about it. I moved away from the city to reduce the risk to everyone else. Now I live up past Rivière- du- Loup. Literally, Wolf River in English. I steer clear of the city at all times. I'm closer to the New Brunswick border. You won't find me though I am hiding in plain sight. Save for one night each month. I head to a forest thick with spruce trees and dark places. Even then, I don't let the wolf run free. At least, not on purpose.

It is in the deepest, coldest part of the woods that I transform. So far, it has killed only deer and moose as there were no headlines in the papers reporting any gruesome findings. I am thinking of crafting a chain like Jacob Marley's and lashing myself to the biggest tree I can find. I don't think the beast will be going anywhere unless it can uproot a very large tree.

I want to live. Just like anyone else, got it? I have taken excruciatingly difficult steps to ensure the wolf is contained on full moon nights. If I exist then others must also. I wish it didn't have to be this way. I wanted to get married and start a family but that isn't to be. A solitary life. At least it is a life, isn't it? I can contribute to society, can't I? It's bad enough that I have to give up on my dreams in order to stay alive and save others from my monster. I'm not cursed. I hate it when people use that term. I don't have a clue how a full moon can turn a man into a monster. I would volunteer for scientific research on werewolves if only such a thing existed.

I don't believe there will ever be a "cure" for my affliction. But maybe there is a way to control the changes somehow. Like, is it possible to only half-change if you have control? What does that half-change look like. Can it be reasoned with? Does it understand language? What are the limitations of its abilities? Are there any?

So many questions waiting to be answered so long as superstition and denial rule people's minds. I was a productive member of society before I was attacked. I wore a badge, and I carried a gun. I shot the monster dead by emptying my automatic into its chest. It took a piece of my left shoulder about the size of a golf ball. I was responding to a routine noise complaint in the industrial section of Sarnia.

Something crossed the path of my cruiser. A flash of grey right past the headlights. I put the car in park and checked in on the radio, then I flashed my light on the new sticky wet snow. There were footprints like I'd never seen before. Each the size of a dinner plate, maybe even a bit larger. That's when I unholstered my weapon and readied myself for an attack as I followed closely.

The attack came. The wolf ... it looked like a wolf, but the damned thing was big. I mean BIG. I didn't hear it coming but I was suddenly on the ground and the werewolf bit into me. I should be dead but for my Kevlar vest. It protected me from getting my arm or neck torn off. I managed to get my weapon in front of me and I emptied the entire clip. The wolf let out a painful sounding yelp and fell into the snow next to me. I shot the damned thing dead and that's when I thought I might be losing my mind because I watched in stunned silence as the creature transformed back into a man.

The flesh of that wolf dissolved. It's the only way I can describe what I saw. Suddenly there were hands and feet where enormous paws used to be. A human face emerged from the last of the dissolving skin and fur. He looked to be in his twenties. Maybe early thirties. There was a big hole in the dead man's chest.

I managed to get back to my cruiser. I was bleeding like a stuck pig, and I stuffed a field dressing underneath my torn Kevlar vest. I grabbed the handset and radioed 'officer down three or four times. It's hard to remember.

That was it. I must have gone into shock. I woke up in the hospital and that's when they went to work on my head by insisting that it was only a man who attacked me. Started making me feel like I was going crazy. I read all I could about werewolves, and I got myself thrown into the jail for the night of the full moon. A cell to myself. Nobody died that night, but all my colleagues on the night shift saw what I was and that was it for my law enforcement career.

To be honest, I'm still a bit amazed that nobody shot me inside that cell."

CHAPTER 7: ANIMAL RIGHTS

For those who choose to believe in the existence of werewolves there are many ethical and moral questions. One must first start with an assumption: that during the period of a full moon an entirely new species of animal will walk the earth killing everything in its path. How much more different is the creature's need to hunt and feed any more different than other predators?

Homosapiens are on the menu for werewolves, but so is pretty much everything else that bleeds. Are these creatures truly monsters from our worst nightmares? Many people think not and have taken to advocating for the rights of those who are host to the creature.

Do Werewolves Need Protection?

"As an activist for animal welfare, we must look at the creatures as something other than monsters. Quite frankly, if we are to believe in the werewolf phenomenon then we must come to terms with the fact that while these creatures are savage, they should have some basic protections afforded to them. What shape these protections take are completely up in the air since very few public intellectuals are prepared to speak on behalf of something that should not exist and those who do speak are labeled as crackpots.

The evidence for the existence of these creatures is irrefutable. Photographs, video, satellite imagery ... oh, don't think for a moment the powers that be haven't tracked the beasts using space-based technology. Perhaps the question of their existence should be put aside in favor of a resounding acknowledgement that werewolves are real, and the truth, as they say, is out there.

The animals have a bad reputation since the Middle Ages because of silly superstitions about demons walking the earth. Maybe they do? Are werewolves one of many earthly incarnations of demonic infiltration into the human world. So, one considers a larger question: Werewolves are real and what are we going to do to protect them and us?"

(Author's note: when confronting the reality of werewolves in our midst the question of what kinds of other terrifying creatures exist in our world consistently comes up. There have been many accounts of monsters, some true, most false and some right out in left field. This is a topic worthy of future research.)

The Creatures Deserve to Hunt in A Controlled Environment

"Look, we can't just expect someone who turns into a werewolf every month to check into a hotel for the night of the full moon. But maybe there is something more palatable where nobody has to die and the creature inside the human being can hunt. A place that is fenced in or protected by a wall of some kind.

(Author's note: I note that it sounds like he is advocating for a dog park for werewolves. He doesn't take my comparison well. That's not to say the idea has no merit, but it would have to be a huge preserve as werewolves can cover a lot of territory in one night.)

"I'm no ethicist and the idea might seem daft to some. I'm an amateur believer in the creatures as I have seen a werewolf stalking through a cemetery during my nighttime security patrols. Yes, I know it sounds made-up, but I am telling you the truth. A huge animal when compared to an actual wolf.

I won't tell you what the thing was doing, digging away at cemetery dirt. Use your imagination. Again, another reason why the creatures deserve to hunt in a controlled environment.

A Reasoned Approach Is Needed

"I'm a psychiatrist and I believe in the werewolf phenomenon after having witnessed a huge wolf-like creature in Cape Breton during a holiday. It was early evening, a full moon. My wife and I had just checked into a quaint bed and breakfast in Port Morien with a breathtaking view of the bay. We had just checked in and unpacked when my wife, standing in front of a picture window said, "Darlene ... look at this. Hurry!" Alarmed by the urgency in her voice, I quickly dropped what I was doing and scrambled over.

When I say that a reasoned approach is needed, I mean it. The werewolf was thundering across the sand at the water's edge no more than a couple of hundred meters away. The bright moon reflected off the waves giving it a shimmering effect.

The first inclination is toward disbelief, and it often shuts down how human beings react to anything inexplicable. But here's the thing: the damned things are real and that's the end of it. The creature splashed across the shore in pursuit of something but neither my wife nor I could see what it was for the life of us.

So, what do you do when you see a wild beast that doesn't fit the description of anything that should be alive? The reasoned approach when faced with something inexplicable is, in my opinion, to gather as many facts as one can in order to better understand what one's eyes are seeing.

That's sort of what I did insomuch as a ten second view of a creature that shouldn't exist. There wasn't time to take a shot or shoot a video of the creature. I would estimate its size to be about the size of a large bear. It didn't walk on two legs, but I have read that a werewolf possesses that ability.

Darlene was the first to call it for what it was. "That's a werewolf," she whispered, astonished. I immediately agreed with her because what I'd just seen didn't fit in my mental archive of large four-legged beasts.

Of course, we heard on the radio news the following morning that police were investigating the discovery of a body inside the town of Port Morien. We found out later through the usual small-town scuttlebutt that the victim, a male, was found mutilated surrounded by large animal prints of an unknown nature.

If werewolves are real and they transform back into their human host at the crack of dawn, then police should be looking for a naked person running around town. They would, no doubt, be covered with blood from the previous evening's hunt. They shouldn't be hard to find if they aren't already dead from someone taking a shot at the creature.

A reasoned approach, to my mind, is to never argue with the physical evidence. You simply mustn't. Physical evidence is much easier for the mind to process. And invoking Occam's Razor, of course.

Legal Standing

"Does that legal standing apply to the period when the human host has transformed into a monster? I don't know if we will ever develop a judicial test for this because to date, no legal authority to my knowledge has ever attempted to prosecute someone who is a werewolf once a month. I don't even know on what grounds charges could be brought against a host.

Surely during the period, they are human it should be expected that extreme protective precautions would be the first thing on their mind? I don't know the answer because I've never met someone who turns into a werewolf. I have seen clear and irrevocable proof of their existence and therefore believe very strongly that werewolves are real, and they are here.

Still, the legal questions are fascinating and if this phenomenon of shape shifting human beings is to be recognized as a genuine occurrence, those questions will need to be answered.

(Author's Note: I ask him for some examples of legal questions.)
Questions? Okay, what is the threshold requirement for 'extreme protective precautions? How do you prove that extreme protective precautions weren't put in place by a host person? What responsibility do they bear when in werewolf form, they only injure a person thereby passing the affliction on?

If a person transforms into a werewolf, what legal standing do they have when the host ceases to be during the full moon each month? They really weren't there, were they? They would have to be conscious of what the creature is doing during the full moon, the human side. How would you prove latency of the creature when it doesn't manifest in the human world between full moons?

And don't forget, to ask a judge these questions mean the subject of werewolves is being heard in a court of law. That's huge. It's massive. It gives the werewolf phenomenon the legitimacy it needs because the creatures are likely more common than we think — they need to be studied. How we do that is entirely up in the air."

Climate Change May Fuel More Attacks

"I work for an environmental organization. We promote education regarding the climate emergency, and we advocate at the community level. We have branches in five Canadian cities now and we're growing. Climate change is a far greater threat than a loup-garou or a werewolf.

We all share this planet. Everything is connected to the overall health of our world. Weather patterns have changed. Winters are much colder. There is a lot more snowfall in central Canada and the Maritimes. Tornadoes more frequent.

These extreme weather events are shaping the world in ways we don't yet completely understand, but if regions are uninhabitable werewolves will always be a part of human migration.

That could lead to a proliferation of the creatures in the inevitable refugee camps that will start popping up. More people mean more prey. More prey means an increased likelihood that some might well survive. One could imagine increases in the werewolf population were this the case."

CHAPTER 8: UNREPENTANT

We have heard from victims and survivors of the werewolf phenomenon. Now it's time to hear from eight hosts to the creature who want the world to know one thing: we have a right to exist. These deeply personal accounts share a sense of frustration over losing possession not only of their bodies for up to twelve hours, but also their very consciousness. At least, the predictability of a werewolf's appearance each month allows for those sufferers to take extraordinary precautions to protect themselves and the creature's prospective prey.

They live in a psychological netherworld, pulled between the creature's mere existence versus that of the host. It's impossible to imagine unless you're living it and the message from these hosts is crystal clear: stay home when the moon is full.

This Is Not My Fault

"I want all of your readers to understand that I don't exactly enjoy turning into the thing that I turn into each month. Though I have no memory of what transpires during the time the werewolf was doing its thing, I know

by the next morning that it couldn't have been particularly good. This is not my fault. People need to understand this. I do everything I can do within reason to put as much distance between the wolf and the prospect of human prey.

Are there some bad hosts? I could answer my own question with another question: are there bad humans out there? Obviously. I am not a host who looks forward to the monster's appearance.

There are other things I would rather be doing with my life than heading thirty miles away from the city and into the bush so as to reduce the risk of a human-monster encounter. Such a meeting can end only one way unless the human is well armed and can shoot a gun faster than the best sharpshooter on the local SWAT team.

I don't ever get into the philosophical questions surrounding the werewolf phenomenon. It's hard for me to be objective and frankly, it angers me that people question my right to exist at all. Look, nobody knows how werewolves come to be, or why. They just are. (*Author's Note: I ask him where he thinks werewolves come from.*)

Where do they come from? Beats the hell out of me. I don't know ... there are all kinds of inexplicable goings-on in our universe.

Look, I turn into a monster every month and I don't have a clue about where it comes from and where it goes to. Maybe it is a curse, who knows? But curse or no curse, there had to be a first werewolf at some point in the past. There needs to be anthropological study of the werewolf phenomenon. Until such time as we understand how the transformation process works, we will never be able to develop a remedy that might shut the process down in its entirety.

All I know is that I am stuck like this. Lots of people believe that I have some moral obligation to end my life because I am a host to a monster. How about no on that one? Everything as a right to exist on this planet the last time I looked. We don't know shit about werewolves, but we could study them. Surely to God some of the smart people you've interviewed for this book of yours advocate letting science guide our understanding of the werewolf phenomenon.

I can't speculate on what makes the werewolf appear. We know that werewolves are contagious. If you are wounded by a werewolf and survive, it's common knowledge that you're going to become a werewolf yourself. I would like for there to be a scientific answer to what I become. I'm raising my hand right now to volunteer for any and all research. I just want my old life back. Is that too much to ask?"

I Have Zero Control Over the Thing Inside Me

"If I could somehow break through into its consciousness, I might be able to gain a measure of control over the thing. That's all I'm asking for. It's like I've been given a superpower, right? Except my superpower is straight up savagery and an unquenchable desire to hunt. I'm a woman under five and a half feet in height. I am young enough to have children. I want a life and I'm willing to do whatever is needed to get rid of the thing inside me. I do mind that I have zero control.

When I was attacked ... the pain was unlike anything I'd ever experienced, and I knew the creature was intent on killing me. I would need a miracle and amazingly, one arrived. Six shots from a police officer's handgun and the monster crashed hard onto the ground a few feet away from me. It rolled onto its side and snuffed a few times. It whimpered, then it became still as a statue. The transformation back to its host began. We were struck dumb at what our eyes were looking at. In seconds there was a dead man laying where a monster had been only seconds ago. He was dead as dead can be and naked.

I've since become friends with the constable. We both know what I am, and he agrees that I have a right to exist. He takes me far away from town and I head into the woods to become the wolf when the full moon makes its presence known. To date, I have not killed a human being. I suspect I would have by now if I didn't have the constable's help each month. If there were a method to exorcise this thing from my body, I would be the first to sign up. Nobody wants to lose control over their body. I just want to be normal again."

I Have Just as Much Right to Exist

"I'm tired of having to explain this because unless you have one of these things in you, then you just don't have a clue what it's like to live this way. Yet there are some who think the werewolf phenomenon is a threat and that if you see one, kill it. That's taking a hell of a substantial risk, by the way, trying to kill a werewolf. A man needs a steady hand and a high muzzle velocity rifle with copper jacketed rounds. Even then, the monster is still a threat. Until it is dead and dissolving back into human form, a werewolf will do everything to continue killing.

But here's one for everyone to chew on, no pun intended. I have a condition that I have no control over. I am a threat for one night a month. But for the other twenty-seven or so days and nights each month, I am the same as anyone else. Because of this, I have just as much right to exist. End of story.

Yes, I know that human beings continue to be killed by those of my kind. Yes, there are hosts that get off on the power and have no problem whatsoever killing human beings. We don't know enough. I don't know if the wolf is listening to our conversation somewhere in a part of my brain where werewolf consciousness resides. If such a thing even exists at all.

But werewolves exist. I've no idea where they come from. I have no idea where they go. I am a vessel for some hidden power the source of which I haven't a clue. But you know what? Whatever, that's what. I am what I have become because I was attacked and survived. I am glad to have survived despite the massive complications hosting a werewolf has on one's life.

One person I communicate with in the United States is a host like me. She's been living this way for more than fifty years now. Knows everything about being a werewolf including how to stash away clothes, so you don't wind up running through the bush naked the following morning. I'm sure I've about ten sweat suits and cheap sneakers. Each package is placed in an easy to find location and its only been a couple of times I had to walk out of the woods with no clothes on.

I should make a note here and tell you that if there was a way to reverse all this and get rid of my monster, I'd be all for it. I want my life back. I want a life. The loneliness one feels because they carry this immense weight. The pressure of knowing that you possess a power, a force so raw that you could rampage through an entire city in one night if the opportunity made itself known.

I do not wish to be a werewolf, but I can't change it, though it has most certainly changed me. I can't even get a dog or a cat because all dogs bark at me now and all cats hiss whenever they see me. Doesn't matter if the dog is a Toy Poodle or an Irish Wolfhound. My roommate is a goldfish. I shit you not. That's me. That's where I'm at now.

The Pain Is Intoxicating

"It's the ultimate high, but you have to let go of yourself. You can't fight the change. Of course, it hurts, every minute of the transformation. Your body is on fire, that's what it feels like at the start. At the same time there is joyous anticipation of the creature's release. Pain and power – dished out in equal measure.

It isn't an exceedingly long high but for the few minutes it exists, there is nothing quite like the feeling of the wolf coursing through your veins. No regrets, no worries, just a wild ride until you disappear.

Waking up inside a freshly scraped hole in the ground. That

or inside someone's open shed. Naked. Cold. Guilt regardless of whether you killed or not. That's the bad part. The good part? For me at least, the pain is intoxicating, even when you wake up shivering you want to go back to the night before and relive the power.

That longing goes away after a day or two. You eat like you're readying yourself for winter hibernation. That lasts a day or two as well.

I have a theory about that. I think the insatiable hunger one feels after the transformation is the body's way of recharging. I mean, your body gets reassembled, twice in less than twelve hours. There's a cost to that. There are all kinds of theories about what this all means, the werewolf phenomenon. It isn't a phenomenon at all. It's a symbiotic relationship between the human body and a power we know little about.

I truly have no regrets. My life's path led me to that terrible night when a werewolf took down half a dozen late-night cross-country skiers at the golf course. I was skiing alone at the time, but it didn't matter. A hundred meters away, six people were butchered by a creature whose sole purpose was to kill in the most graphic way imaginable.

I skied for my life. In no time the creature was on me. It slashed me from the base of my neck all the way down to my tailbone. I remember a bright spotlight coming from a snowmobile. Then gunshots.

The werewolf abandoned me, and I didn't see what happened to it because I blacked out due to blood loss. I woke up in the hospital in Charlottetown. My wounds healed up fast. Less than a week in care and then discharged.

So, it's a crap shoot, right? Either believe it was a werewolf or don't. I chose to believe. It's what frames everything that I do now. Knowing that I am not entirely human anymore. That doesn't give me (or any host) the right to kill human beings. I have built a solitary life in the brief time since I became a host. Less than two years.

(Author's note: I ask if he as killed a human, and he ended the conversation.)

I Have No Memory of The Monster's Night

"I have hosted the wolf now for going on a decade. *The Floating Boar* incident. Happy hour extended well past 7:00 PM that night. I was there with a couple of other girls. Around half-past seven is when the screaming began. Jesus, it was awful. Patrons crushed trying to get to the doorway. The monster: I'd never seen anything move so fast in my life. It made its way to the kitchen and spotted me.

It came at me in a burst of salivating fury. That's when my so-called friends decided to disappear into the mad rush leaving me alone with a big ass wolf. It ripped into my leg with a slash of its razor-sharp claws. Not like fishnet would do any good. Strangely, the monster took a sharp left when I thought for certain I'd be torn apart like everyone else. That miracle bought me a few seconds to find a better place to hide. I limped past the still twitching bodies of the line cook and his two short order cooks. Intestines and organs everywhere. I slipped but managed to steady myself.

I slid into the walk-in fridge. I locked the door with the metal peg and thankfully one of the staff members had left a plaid coat laying on a box of avocados. I slipped my arms inside and zipped it up. Then I took a quick look at the back of my left leg. It was bleeding badly, and I remembered my first aid. I found a roll of plastic bags on a shelf next to a box of latex gloves. I slapped on a tourniquet with a twisted up back. I tied the tightest knot I could to slow the bleeding. I looked down to see the bleeding was under control. Little did I know that I was now host to my own creature and gosh darn it, the wolf would be making its debut in twenty-eight days. Awesome.

They discharged me after two days in general care. This after a grilling from the police about what happened at The Floating

Boar. I didn't go back to the job for obvious reasons. My head was full of bad dreams for a week after the attack. I saw my wolf in my mind's eye and it saw me. We took a good hard look at each other, like we were sizing each other up.

I owned land up near Wawa. Nothing but forest as far as the eye can see. The cabin was about two miles off the beaten path. I parked my Jeep in front of the cabin and then remembered there was a root cellar with a separate entrance. I could lock myself inside with a chain and a good padlock. The door would have to withstand against a monster that I knew little about. I found a brand-new combination lock (meaning older than dirt but still in the original packaging) and about three feet of chain in the shed. I threw the chain over my shoulder and grabbed the lock. Then I headed back to the root cellar and chained myself in, committing the combination of the lock to memory.

The pain of the transformation hit me at around 9 PM. I had spent the past three hours locked inside the root cellar pacing back and forth in the darkness. I have no memory of the monster's night. All I remember was the closest experience I'd ever been to feeling my entire body on fire. I remember seeing my feet break and then reform in a matter of seconds. I screamed the entire time. My head felt like it was going to explode like an over-filled balloon.

That's all I remember of that first change. I woke up on a dirt floor covered with claw marks. The door, a heavy wooden door with metal on both sides. Nothing but scrapes and scratches from the monster attempting to dig its way to freedom. But the lock worked. I was safe, naked, and cold. I survived the night, and I contained the creature. I had a month to reinforce the root cellar. I have also recorded the transformation on one of those little destruction-proof cameras.

(Author's note: I asked if anyone else had seen it and she declined to answer. I didn't witness her transformation, but I believe her story.)

Precautions

"You can only do so much. You can only take the most reasonable steps as a precaution to protect human beings, their pets, their livestock. You do this unless you're a bent asshole who gets off on killing. Anything warm blooded that crosses my wolf's path is a goner. I don't want to kill anyone or anything.

I don't know how many people like me that you've talked with, but I have to believe that most people who carry the wolf inside don't want to kill anyone or anything. As terrifying as the monster is, people forget that this apex predator also has a target on its back. You kill it, you kill me. I don't want to die anytime soon. I'm only twenty-eight for crying out loud. I can count on one hand how many serious relationships I've been in. None since the attack. None for the rest of my life no doubt.

I was in the wrong place at the wrong time. I didn't hear it or see it coming. I was liquored up big time and decided to walk home to my apartment. I was only five blocks from my place, and I made the stupid decision to cut across a darkened parking lot. That's when it came for me. Who could ever forget seeing something that big and ferocious? That's the kind of terror that can make a man shit his pants when you see it for the first time.

As with all human hosts, I've no idea what my wolf looks like, but I've survived an attack. I know first-hand how bloody terrifying these creatures are because one tried to eat me. It was huge. Twice the height and width of a Great Dane. Shaggy grey and black fur. Blood all around its muzzle and into its fur. I remember the smell of its breath in my face. It dug its claws into my shoulders and that's when I started screaming because that was it for yours truly.

Miracle of miracles, just as the werewolf was going to tear my throat out, a car pulled into the parking lot with the music just blaring like mad. And then the car started doing donuts. I don't think the driver saw me or the wolf yet, but the strangest thing happened. As I lay on the asphalt, smoke from the burning tires blanked the lot. Not much worse smelling than burned rubber. The monster took a dislike to the smoke or maybe it was the deafening screeching of the tires. It was on me one second and gone the next. I don't know what happened to it after that. I woke up in hospital; nurses all marveling at how fast my wounds healed. Save for one. She whispered in my ear, 'I know what you are.' It was chilling. I got the hell out of there ASAP.

The fact is, I should be dead and I'm very much alive."

There Are Other Creatures That Like to Feed on Human Beings

"The creature runs on a built-in need to hunt, kill and eat. Human beings are easy prey and yet are far more complex creatures than a mere wild dog. Our survival instincts have dulled over the centuries thanks to industrialization. It is far easier now, in our age of wireless devices, to order supper on your phone than to use it to grow your knowledge of how to protect yourself against something that won't stop hunting and killing until first light. Look, human beings are a food group. Do you understand?

There are multitudes of creatures on the planet that are quite happy to kill people. There are more than five hundred fatalities each year resulting from hippopotamus attacks. We don't yet know how many victims are butchered by werewolves each year. You have to think it's less than killer hippos.

Obviously, there are other creatures that look to feed on human beings. Not just werewolves, though they might well be the most ferocious. Creatures natural and unnatural. Natural predators are bears and lions and crocodiles. I am host to a werewolf; I am an unnatural being. I believe there must be other unnatural creatures in existence.

(Author's Note: I ask what kinds of creatures. He was very matter of fact.)

What kinds? Well, that's something I can't be certain of. Do zombies dig themselves out of the grave to eat people's brains? No. But in every city, bodies have been found to be completely exsanguinated. A werewolf eats its prey in a wild manner. Something else must exist that drains its victims of their blood. You're right, I'm calling it. Vampires exist.

Who really knows what else, right? Demons in human form? They've always been with us. Once upon a time we didn't even question the existence of the unnatural. It was a given that werewolves walked the earth along with other deadly creatures.

Flash-forward five hundred years and we've been to the moon. We've touched the outer reaches of the solar system. Science is the new god for some. It's just not compatible with unnatural creatures because science has yet to accept their existence let alone explain them. There absolutely must be a scientific reason why these monsters exist. If we can't find one, then all we have left is superstition and legends to go by. I know there must be more to the story. I feel compassion for those people who wind up hosting the creature. I don't know what the answer is, but we need to start somewhere."

CHAPTER 9: FOUND FOLKLORE

The following are old stories and firsthand accounts from witnesses, survivors, and human hosts. They come from across the country, different time periods each, but similar stories to modern witness accounts. We tend to think of The Werewolf Phenomenon as akin to spinning silk into gold: pure fantasy.

It's easy to understand why most people take a dim view of what they believe to be superstitious nonsense in our technology-driven, wirelessly connected world. Yet it is those very wireless devices that makes it harder and harder to keep the truth at bay.

The creatures predate modern technology, but that didn't stop people from recording their terrifying encounters with these most fierce predators. Human beings have always passed down knowledge through story and music. In many cases, it is folklore can offer clues to the mystery behind werewolves.

The Beast in The Boxcar

From a letter postmarked at Thunder Bay in 1896.

Dearest Mother:

I must tell you about a most fantastic and terrifying experience I had recently. I was working the switches at Field and my lantern was glowing brightly. The night was clear and warm and the smell of wood burning in the handful of nearby homes had me thinking about my own home, hence the letter.

As I lined up the switches for an inbound train coming out of the spiral tunnels, I heard the most ungodly howling coming from a sidetrack with a dozen or so boxcars waiting to be added to incoming and outgoing trains. A powerful, rage-filled howl the likes of which I have not heard in my short life. I am used to the sound of wolves howling when the night is clear and cold. This was no wolf, and I hadn't even gone to investigate yet. Some things are warnings to steer clear. In hindsight we probably should have given what we saw and heard inside that boxcar.

This small train station is little more than a tiny dot on a ribbon of steel cut through the Canadian wilderness. Wildlife encounters are common as elk roam the tracks when the trains have run through. Grizzly bears are often seen as one rolls down the hill from the tunnels into our tiny village.

The howling was such that I went to investigate along with another switchman. Four boxcars in and we found the source of the roaring. We held out our lamps and saw the boxcar had a seal on it. Winnipeg. Then, the entire boxcar started to shake as the howling turned into a feral sounding roar.

Worse than you can imagine than even the angriest lion or tiger. Scratching and scraping at the thick wooden walls of the boxcar, like it was trying to dig its way out. My partner had a gun, again, handy when you work in the wilderness.

"Open it up," he said, taking aim.

I waved him away. "Don't be ridiculous, for all we know the beast in the boxcar is someone's circus animal. Or perhaps it is going to the new zoo they are building out west."

He lowered his weapon and gave me a shrug as the boxcar continued to shake and vibrate as the creature, whatever it was, wanted the hell out of there. Period.

I held up the lantern just above a gap between the slats of wood and chanced a peek.

I don't mind telling you that what I saw, I shall never forget. It was a beast from the pits of hell. The fiercest looking animal I had ever seen. Thick fur brushed against my face as I stepped back from the boxcar. Suddenly a wolf-like snout and huge white teeth pushed against the gap in the wood. It began chewing on the wood and that's when my partner and I turned and ran back to the bunkhouse.

We locked the doors and turned down the coal lantern in case the wolf-thing managed to escape. I grabbed a rifle and put one up the spout. The sky was turning pink in the east and the sun would be up within the hour.

The howling continued unabated for another thirty minutes. It ended abruptly as soon as the sun poked its face just above the mountains. We went to investigate. No longer was the boxcar shaking. We looked inside to see a naked man curled up in a corner. That was enough for me.

A beast that changed back into a man as soon as the sun came up. I count my blessings now because I have seen the Devil and he is as real as you or me. (Author's Note: This is where the letter ends.)

Sod House Journal

April 10, 1901:

I have decided to keep a journal as James, and I begin to work the land we received on a grant from the Canadian Pacific Railway. We are from Northern England. This place is so alien to me. We are but a tiny speck in an ocean of near treeless land that goes on for days and days and days, interrupted by the occasional river valley. Our place is near Ellisboro, inside a valley.

The soil is good, James tells me. We have time still to break ground and dig a garden beside our home: a sod house that we built from the earth beneath our feet and with our bare hands. The garden will be easier, because we will be digging in the same spot where we cut the turf for our home. We will of course, hope for good rains. We are lucky in that we can draw water from the stream, but I boil it just to be on the safe side. My husband as even caught a few fish there. I believe the space for the garden will be large enough to provide potatoes, carrots, beets, and turnips to get us through the winter. I mustn't forget to plant peas and green beans.

The well is freshly dug. The water smells like sulfur. Boiling it does little to eliminate the foul odor. I have a small cast iron stove which heats our tiny one-room home. It isn't much. I feel most days as if we landed on another world entirely, but James always lifts my spirits and I do have my beloved piano.

It is from the middle of nowhere in this flat ocean of prairie that I must recount the most amazing encounter during the last full moon. It's almost too fantastic to be believed and by rights James and I should be dead. We heard the howling first. Unlike any sound I've *ever heard before. Mad. Raging. It was enough to send me dashing back into the soddy for the shotgun and the carbine. In seconds I was back outside next to James. I handed him the carbine and then readied the shotgun.*

I remember thinking there must be an enormous bear near our sod house, and I asked James if he thought it might be a bear. He shook his head as he held out the lantern, the carbine tucked under his left shoulder. Yellow-orange light poured out of our tiny house in the middle of nowhere. Then ... a god forsaken roar mixed in with screams like that of terrified sheep. The full moon cast a blue-grey glow across the prairie and perhaps a hundred yards from our sod house we spotted it. And it spotted us. Standing atop a freshly killed pronghorn. The beast was no bear. It was no creature I had ever seen in my life, and it was coming for James and me.

He took aim and fired round after round. The wolf, that's what I believe it was. A demon wolf. It kept on coming. I fired two shots from the shotgun just as James fired another volley at the creature. We hit it repeatedly. Enough to make the monster turn tail and run. I do not know what happened to it. At sunrise, James and I followed a trail of enormous wolf prints into a meadow. It was there we saw the butchered carcasses of eight pronghorns. I believe that if we hadn't shot the monster to pieces, we would have ended up like those pronghorns. Dear Lord, what kind of land is this?

Samuel de Champlain's Lucky Shot

The following account has been translated from a seventeenth century manuscript found in a North Bay Ontario home in 1917. The document is dated shortly after the death of the founder of New France in 1635 and has been translated into English.

"My name is Emil Pelletier and I hereby give a full account of Samuel de Champlain's encounter with a loup-garou in the area of the Ottawa River in 1613 as was told to me by my father who was with the great man that day. My father was a simple tracker and laborer as well as an excellent hunter. His job was to keep the men fed which wasn't a hard thing to do as the forests were swimming with

wild game.

Rabbit, deer, moose, elk, even black bear. All were plentiful as was fresh fish from any of the thousands of clean, cold streams and rivers that had to be crossed as the famous explorer charted his daily progress.

Full moon in October 1613. A howl on the cold night air that shakes the trees and tiny leaves fall to the ground. Whatever made the sound was close by. My father said that you could hear the creature's breathing as it moved in and out of the shadows nearest the camp.

"That is no wolf!" de Champlain pronounced with the authority of a man who has brought down the most dangerous of game. My father loaded Samuel de Champlain's gun and handed it to the man. Then he threw a torch out in the vicinity of where the animal breathing was coming from.

The torch landed on its side casting an amber glow across the forest floor, touching the feet of the monster. It was standing on its legs, and it had one of our men's heads in its sharp-toothed mouth. That is when Samuel de Champlain opened fire on the creature sending it spinning like a top. My father handed another loaded gun, and another shot was fired. The ball hit the creature in the center of its chest. It tumbled backward, tripping over its feet and landing face first in the dirt.

Another loaded gun and Samuel de Champlain took a step forward as my father tossed another torch. It landed closer this time and that is when the horror of the night began. The wolf began to waste away. Great clumps of fur melted off the creature's body as it twisted and contorted in a series of violent jerks. The muzzle and the razor-sharp teeth fell off the dead man's face like wet clay.

There before Samuel de Champlain and my father, was a dead man. A French laborer that my father knew in the days before the creature attacked. My father said the man believed himself to be cursed. It is a demon that takes a man's soul and transforms him into a giant wolf when the moon is full. It is the demon's hunger the fuels the beast.

I can confirm that Samuel de Champlain was brave and decisive in confronting the creature as it was my father's pleasure to serve in his party of explorers."

A Ghost Walks Silently

Diary Entry for Matthew Carol

April 13, 1811:

I believe that because the almighty gives us free will to follow him in faith that his grace protects good Christian men, even to the wars against Napoleon. Too many sailors and soldiers have been killed and maimed in these terrible wars of conquest. So many ghosts. I have seen them. Any man can see them if he only lets his eyes look upon that which terrifies him so. A ghost walks silently, forever holding vigil over the place where it breathed its last. A murderous creature from Hell also walks silently as it stalks it human prey.

What we saw, what was ready to attack Darcy and me, We didn't even give ourselves time to do any other than kill the vile monster. Yes, a monster. Not a man monster. No, this was an enormous creature resembling a wolf. A horrendous mixture of man and beast. A wolf-man walking silently on four legs or two.

I fired on the creature as did my mate Darcy. Both lead balls found their way into the creature's flesh. It tumbled into a wall and tried to get back up onto its feet. We shot the beast one more time. It emitted a weak sounding moan and then fell onto its side and died.

Then we witnessed the horror. A beast transformed into a man I knew from the pub. A rowdy bastard according to Darcy. Well, rowdy or not, we killed a wolf-man that night and I shall never forget it.

Kamloops Work Crew

I was in Kamloops night of that full moon. The night one of the new fellas, this guy was from Williams Lake. Kept mostly to himself. He drank far too much for anyone's good. But drink and drink and drink and drink he did. Round about four in the afternoon he started shouting like an escaped lunatic. "Run for your lives! Before the full moon. Run for your lives!"

He staggered around the entire work camp; a bottle of rot gut in one hand and a piece of bread in the other. Shouting his warning the entire time. And, to me at least, there was genuine belief in his voice. A sense of urgency despite his drunken state. It raised the hair on the back of my neck. I decided to pull up stakes and hit the road because I had a bad feeling about that crazy drunk.

What I heard that night. Indeed, what everyone heard was the kind of howling that can only come from a place where God had no business. My mind flashed, strangely, to the pictures of medieval woodcut prints. Some of the images showed huge wolves that could walk on their back legs like a human. They would steal sheep and devour shepherds.

Well, I caught a clear look at the source of the howling. It was maybe three hundred yards away and even from that distance, the monster was enormous. It tore toward us, and God help anything that crossed its path. Then a loud *CRACK!*. The thing fell dead before it could take another step. Do I believe in werewolves? Absolutely. Absolutely.

A Monster's Journal

Author's Note: the following is a deeply personal account from a new host as he questions whether there is anywhere in a civilized world where a monster can go and not hurt anyone.

January 16th

It is the coldest, darkest time of year. My monster revels in the snow and frigid temperatures. I will often see the remains of my monster's kills. Head torn off. Blood-stained snow in all directions and tremendous footprints.

I remember placing my right hand into one of the footprints; trying, perhaps, to conjure up even the tiniest memory from the hunt. As always, I came up with nothing. The footprint is three times as large as my hand.

Where do I disappear to when the wolf is free? Where is the wolf right now, this moment as I write these words? I am forsaken because of my monster. This despite knowing my prayer book backward and forward. I worship with my neighbors in a tiny country church.

I do not believe that God hears my prayers. The wolf is a demon from hell. Why should God care about me? Perhaps I am damned for all time. I wear a silver cross. It has no effect on my transformation. I head to the forest in the morning of the change. I don't stop walking until the sun is low on the western horizon. Then I know I am deep enough in the wilderness that my monster becomes just another predator. It is a delicate balance.

How can I find love with this curse? How can I hope to have children? How can I hope at all? What is the purpose of my affliction? Am I to be shot to death like the creature who wounded me? Is that the best ending to life that a man can hope for?"

In The Aftermath

Author's note: below is another example of found folklore. The story, dated from the early 1800's in Upper Canada, offers a compelling view of a new host in the weeks after surviving a werewolf attack. Whether it is a true story remains unclear, but the details are uncanny.

It was such that her nightmares began to seep into her daytime thoughts. She shouldn't be alive, she, the daughter of a good family. The daughter who was to be married except her intended was no longer breathing.

"That's right," she said, leaning up in her feather bed. "The beast killed him and then attacked me. I survived. That's what happened."

She replayed it repeatedly in her mind. The carriage came to a sudden stop. The horses reared up and the carriage tipped onto its side. An enormous wolf slashed the neck of one terrified horse while ripping the throat out from the other horse with its long sharp teeth. She watched in horror as the monster tore open the driver with one powerful rip from its sharp claws and his guts spilled out.

Her intended loaded his gun and crawled out from the wreck. He hadn't enough time to aim, and she saw his end as the creature slashed her lover's face. Then it began to dig into his chest and tear out his organs. The gun, fell out of the man's hands as he screamed for God to take him quickly, all the while the beast fed as he died.

The daughter would be next if she didn't do something to save her life. She scrambled out from under the carriage and pulled the gun from the dead driver's hands. Terrified, she brought the weapon to her shoulder and fired a ball that tore an enormous chunk of flesh from the monster's chest.

The wolf spun around quickly, saliva and blood dangling from its lips. It slashed her across her breasts, tearing the expensive fabric and cutting into her smooth ivory flesh. The daughter blacked out after that. It was all she could remember of the night when she lost her man and lost her future happiness.

She should have died for loss of blood, but another coach found her amid the bloody carnage. They patched her up and she awoke in her bed; her left arm bound tightly across her chest. It hurt to breathe. It hurt to move little more than a finger.

"H-He died," she whispered as a tear rolled down her left cheek. "They all died but me. but how? It was a monster. A wolf."

Priests and police did their very best to convince her that she and her fiancée had been attacked by a naked mad man. They even showed her the body, including the large ball hole in his chest. "It was a huge wolf that I shot and not a man," she would insist to their collective frustration.

The father came to take her to the country house. Away from the city with its dirty streets and foul air. "You were lost to us for more than a week, but you came back," the father said with an air of relief in his voice. "You have healed up remarkably well, the doctors tell me. They'd never seen wounds heal so quickly."

She felt a painful burning sensation across her breasts. From deep inside the very scars that had grown over the wounds to her chest and neck since the night of the attack. But her attacker was not a mad man, of that she was certain. She decided to remind her father that it was the biggest wolf she had ever seen that attacked her carriage.

"It was a wolf that killed everyone but only wounded me," she said with dead certainty in her voice. "I shot it in the chest, and it died."

The father reached across the coach and took his daughter's hand. "My dearest if it had been a wolf there would have been a carcass. What we found instead of a dead wolf was a naked man shot to death in the manner you just described."

What about the dead horses?" she snapped, angry that her father was talking to her like an infant. "A mad man just killed two large horses with his bare hands. He tore the throat out of one. He butchered the driver and my fiancée, utterly mutilating their bodies. You wish me to believe this is what happened, father?"

She pulled her hand away and her father, lowered his gaze because he knew right from the start that no mad man could have butchered large livestock with his bare hands. Everything his daughter said was correct because he had seen the large wolf prints around and underneath the body of the naked man. No human footprints were to be seen anywhere near the dead man. So, how could a mad man have found his way without leaving a single footprint? It wasn't possible, but that is what the father decided to make himself believe.

"Then I am to believe that you will turn into a large wolf the next full moon as legend suggests?" he asked, not unkindly. "Perhaps it is best that we be in the country should you transform into a wolf. There is nothing but woodland and wildlife for miles. Any sharp-toothed creature would be glad to hunt there, I'd say."

He smiled at this daughter the best way that a worried father could. It didn't help.

"If I am a wolf, father, then you should leave me to my fate because I cannot guarantee that I wouldn't kill or maim you, mother or anyone in the family. How can I be alive, father? I should be dead, yet the wounds have nearly healed, and my mind is filled with horrible images of the dead. There was so much blood, father."

"It was your quick thinking that saved your life then," the father said soothingly "Rest now as there are many more hours of travel ahead."

The coach offered a comfortable ride and the father fortified them both against any the chill with a flask of whisky. It warmed her insides enough that she smiled for the first time in weeks. She took another sip from her father's flask and then leaned against the window and fell asleep.

Cobblestones. The werewolf's massive claws tore at the mortar kicking up chunks of stone. A cold breeze blew against the beast's face carrying with it the scent of nearby prey. In seconds it was on them; a trio of drunks staggering up a narrow alley.

It went for the one in the middle; the she-wolf's enormous jaws clamped down on the man's neck as blood filled her mouth and poured down her throat. With a sharp pull, she tore the man's head off. Then she went for the two remaining men who were running for their lives. The beast lunged just as one of the men tripped over his own feet and tumbled across the wet stones.

Her wolf, her beast, the feral rage. She embraced as the power of the creature surged through her newly transformed body. The deadly predator slashed the man's back and ripped his right arm clean at the shoulder. The last man was chased up a narrow alleyway. The last drunk. Easy prey. She was silent as she backed him against a brick wall. He drunkenly kicked at the creature only to watch his shoe fly off his foot.

With a roar, she dispatched the man with a slash across his neck that tore so deeply into the flesh, the man's head dangled over his left shoulder, held only by a flap of skin. Blood gushed from the man's neck as his mostly headless body dropped to the bricks like a sack of wet sand. The she-wolf fed at its leisure, its glowing eyes glancing up at the full moon every few seconds.

The daughter opened her eyes. She gazed out at through the window. "I dreamed of hunting three men," she said in a tired voice. "I killed them, and the dream replayed itself repeatedly. I learned that I wanted the dream to continue,"

Unsure what to say or do, the father nodded sympathetically. The daughter sat in silence as the coach bumped over the uneven road. She gazed out the window occasionally and would see a deer bolt out of the bush or a pheasant fly out from its roost.

She quickly sat to attention as something outside the coach had caught her eye. "Stop the coach please, I need to get some air." She shouted it loud enough for the driver to hear and in seconds the coach was rolling to a gentle stop.

"What's wrong?" the father asked, sounding alarmed at her tone. "Why are we stopping?"

The daughter stepped out quickly and started marching toward a clearing in the woods. She spotted them following the coach not long ago. Three gray wolves.

"Stay here," she shouted back to the driver and her father.

The daughter reached the clearing and continued walking for a few seconds. She stretched out both arms with her palms facing the sky and closed her eyes. She could hear the trio of wolves approaching through the tall grass. The breeze whooshed gently across the treetops amid the echo of birdsong. If the wolves wanted, they could have taken her down. Instead, the three stopped an arm's length away and sat down like any well-trained dog. The daughter knelt as the three wolves sniffed and licked her hands.

The burning sensation from within the scars on her chest ceased as if by some miraculous intervention. One of the wolves emitted a soft whine as it stepped forward and licked the daughter's face.

"Good wolf," she whispered. "Good wolf

10: THREE SAVAGE STORIES

While strictly fiction (to the best of the author's knowledge) the following stories demonstrate the true brutality of a werewolf attack. There can be no argument: werewolves are simply the most dangerous creatures on four legs or two. Survivors and witnesses have long said they experienced a kind of primal fear after hearing the beast howl.

Of course, a person is going to hide and hope that the monster circling them in the snow moves on but that isn't to be. Flee? But to where? A huge predator is hunting you and you're going to die in the next few minutes. Where can you run? It can smell a pin drop of your sweat from miles away.

Human beings record their experiences in a multitude of ways. Storytelling, true or otherwise is just a continuation of what our species has always done throughout recorded history.

Late Night Diner

Six people occupied the late-night diner. Four of the six ate there three times a week after driving short hauls between Toronto and London. The server and the cook made up the other two. Outside, the temperature had plummeted and there was frost on the sidewalk.

"Mike, we need to throw some salt on the sidewalk," the server shouted as she poured the four truckers' fresh coffee.

"Yup," the cook answered. "Hey, Denise, why is it that I'm the one to do the sidewalk?"

The long-time server slid the glass carafe onto its heating element. "Because you're the big strong man, that's why."

Ah," said the cook with a shrug. He grasped the metal handle on the bucket of salt that was in the storeroom. Inside was a metal scoop. He pushed through the kitchen doors, deciding it wouldn't take more than a minute to complete.

"Thank you," Denise called out.

Mike stepped outside. He unsnapped the lid and pulled up a big scoop of salt which he quickly tossed on the sidewalk to his right. Hundreds of tiny rock crystals scattered across the concrete. He repeated the procedure for the sidewalk to his left and then shivered for a second as he gazed up at the full moon.

That was the moment it made its presence known. Mike the cook should have hightailed it back into the restaurant and locked the doors, instead he stood there, struck dumb by what he was seeing. The creature, a sharp-toothed monster. Hundreds of pounds of deadly animal flesh sprinted across the empty parking lot and Mike the cook had barely enough time to choke out a scream before the huge werewolf dove on him and began tearing through his flesh. A gusher of blood splashed onto the beast's muzzle and its chest.

Then it howled over its fresh kill. Inside the restaurant the four truckers bolted from their booth as Denise dropped her tray of dirty dishes. The wolf tore into Mike's back with fangs and sharp claws, and it began to feed. Denise stifled a horrified scream and ran for her life to the diner's entry. She secured the restaurant by locking the doors. Then she shut the lights off.

"There's a monster outside," she whispered. "It killed … It killed, Mike."

Neither of the short haul truckers had a chance to utter a single word. A pane of glass imploded into dagger-like shards. The werewolf landed on the floor a few feet away from the truckers. It was here where they would spend their last few moments on Earth.

All four men started backing away toward the kitchen, their hands out in front of their bodies for protection. One pulled a huge hunting knife from a sheath in his boot. The werewolf wasn't picky. It raised itself onto his rear legs and suddenly the monster was nearly eight feet tall. It took a step forward and then another as its beastly growl rumbled through the near empty diner. The trucker with a knife waited until the wolf was a couple of arms lengths away when he launched his attack on the fur covered beast. He'd always kept the blade razor sharp. It cut through the creature's thick fur and muscle tissue, embedding itself to the hilt in the monsters left shoulder.

Enraged, the wolf swiped at the one who'd thrown the knife. The one who fought back. The man's head flew off and landed on the still piping hot grill with one powerful swipe of the beast's right forepaw. Blood and human flesh seared with a loud hiss immediately upon contact with the grease-soaked hot metal plate. The smoke—it would have made the remaining three truckers throw up if they weren't already fighting for their lives.

Denise scrambled from behind the counter with a long soup ladle in her hand. She swept the trucker's partially cooked head onto the floor, and it landed with a hollow thud. She threw up into a garbage can as the werewolf punched into the second trucker's chest. Its huge left claw came out the other side with a pair of torn lungs and a shredded heart. The corpse twitched a few times as the creature let it slide onto a blood and bile-soaked floor.

The monster backed the last two truckers into a corner. Their huge eyes; surprised, shocked, terrified. Both men quickly looked at each other and then ran, the pair of them straight into the rear legs of the monster. They hit with enough force to send the creature tumbling. That was unexpected. It dug its sharp claws into the black and white tile floor, scraping to a stop.

It slowly raised itself onto its rear legs and the server noticed the creature had a long scar down the center of its belly. From neck to navel. And she remembered her late husband and how he wore the same scar after his open-heart surgery. He'd been gone five years, taken far too soon by a heart attack even though he'd had a triple bypass.

With a pair of strikes, the monster's claws tore through the remaining two truckers' plaid shirts and deep into their abdomens. Both men looked down to see their bowels splashing onto the floor. It held down one corpse with its huge front left paw and fed on the other man's chest.

Denise knew death was certain if she didn't think fast. There were a lot of sharp objects in the kitchen. Knives of every shape and description she could hurl at the monster. What she needed was to hurt it, beyond the stab wound that appeared to have miraculously healed. Her eyes quickly panned over to the deep fryer. The oil was hot enough to cause third degree burns. She grabbed a pot with a long handle and quickly dipped it in the fryer.

The werewolf turned toward the kitchen as the petrified server stepped around the corner and splashed the burning hot oil right into the monster's eyes. The beast staggered backwards shrieking and clawing at its face and tearing its flesh. Denise took another few seconds to reload the pot with more hot oil. Once again, she stepped around the corner and splashed the oil into the creature's eyes for a second time.

It tripped over a table and fell hard on its back. Surrounding the beast was the bloody evidence of its short visit to the late-night diner. Four dead truckers, and outside, Mike the cook. Each cut to bits by something from hell.

The server, the last person alive. She'd hurt the monster. She didn't panic and kept her head, but the werewolf was far from done. It rolled over and back up to all fours and sniffed the air. Its eyes: nothing more than burn and blister. The werewolf could no longer see until the healing completed, but even temporary blindness could not stop the beast from hunting. It turned toward the kitchen and scrambled clumsily in the direction of the scent of living flesh. The entire time the creature's stomach rumbled, even as it slipped and crashed all over the blood covered tiles.

The server filled the pot with hot grease a final time and splashed it on the monster's face. The beast recoiled and clawed at its face with nails shaped like shark's teeth. Blood poured through the now open wounds as the server dashed to the back of the kitchen and out the rear door. Denise ran for her life to her car and dove behind the wheel. In seconds she was on her phone with the police.

"H-Huge wild animal," she said, breathless. "Inside Cross-Town Diner. Everybody is dead. So much blood. Dear God, save us."

The scalding hot oil melted the monster's eyes inside their sockets. There was no coming back from that for the beast or for its human host. From the safety of her car, the server watched in horror as the enormous blind monster crashed and tripped over the freshly dead.

A voice in the server's head told her to record the scene with her phone. Smartly, Denise listened to that voice and quickly began to record the video evidence of what murdered

Mike the short order cook and four of her late-night regulars who wouldn't have hurt a fly. In the distance she could hear sirens. She quickly saved the video file on her phone, but she also backed it up to her online storage that she got for free with the new laptop last Christmas. She knew the police would confiscate her phone. She deleted the app for the online storage as well as her social media and her email apps.

The first two police cars arrived on opposite ends of the street and parked in a position to block approaching traffic. Another police cruiser pulled up in front of the restaurant, sliding to a halt of the frost covered asphalt. The twenty-year veteran was behind the wheel, Sergeant Parker. His charge was a fresh from the academy rookie on only his fourth night shift.

"You see what I'm seeing, kid?" the sergeant asked as he pulled the shotgun from its rack.

The rookie, Constable Jelinek. It took a moment for what he was looking at to register.

"In the doorway, Jesus God. Sergeant … that's a freaking werewolf!" the young officer choked.

The veteran who'd thought he'd seen it all decided to treat the raging monster the way he would treat a rabid dog. You had to kill it.

"Listen up, kid," he said hiding the worry in his voice because he was pretty sure his protégé was bang on. Werewolf, angry bear, it didn't matter. "Whatever it is, we need to take it down because there's more dead in the restaurant according to dispatch. Turn on your body camera."

The rookie officer did as he was instructed as they exited the cruiser. They stepped around and over what was left of Mike the short order cook. Inside the restaurant, unnatural growling that the young officer felt in his fillings.

Crashing sounds and the crunch of broken glass. Both officers got a good look at what had caused the sheer butchery inside and outside that late night diner.

"Alright, get ready," the veteran said. "This is going to be the first time you ever fired your weapon in a tactical situation. Follow my lead. Center of visible mass. Only enough rounds to drop it. Any questions?"

Constable Jelinek's head bobbed up and down in a near blur. "No, Sergeant."

He patted him on a shoulder tucked with an inch of Kevlar. The vests would save their lives, the Sergeant thought. He'd read about the werewolf phenomenon and stories of survivors who wore body armour.

"Alright," he cocked the shotgun. "Only enough rounds to drop it. Not a round extra. Let's do this."

He pushed open the door and the bell rang. The werewolf, the massive creature stood on two legs and turned toward the sound of the chime. It could no longer see but it surely could smell them. Two people. Sweat. Warm blood.

The monster did what the monster always would do. What it existed for. To hunt. To kill. To feed. And then hunt some more. Hunt and hunt and hunt until the first signs of dawn at which time it would crawl off to a quit dark place and fall asleep until the next hunt on the next full moon.

It scrambled and smashed its way blindly toward the officers. Blood and saliva dripped from its lips in long thin tendrils. It knew how close it needed to be to make a kill. Two more steps and then it could unleash its visceral rage.

"Fire," the police sergeant shouted. He squeezed the trigger and put a 12-gauge pattern all over the monster's chest. Blood and fur dripped to the floor as the wound was deep and wide. The rookie fired three shots from his Glock into the animal's chest, all three of which penetrated the heart and lungs. The monster reared up one final time and then tripped over one of the mutilated bodies. It hit the ground hard and did not get up. A few seconds later, it stopped breathing.

As the transformation began, both officers lowered the weapons. The werewolf's face, badly scarred began dissolving into a gelatinous substance that dripped off the human body beneath the monster. Claws fell onto the dirt and dissolved. Its long truck split up the middle with a sticky sound and then transformed into more of the disgusting goo.

"This can't be happening, Sergeant," the rookie sounded like he was about three seconds away from losing his shit.

"It's on camera," the veteran officer said. "It's happening. It's also dead. And so is the person underneath. I'm calling it in."

The diner remained closed for the next few days as investigators pieced together what happened. It was obvious from the fact that bloody wolf prints littered the restaurant that an animal was responsible for the carnage. An animal with a long scar on its chest and belly, just like the scar on the dead man's chest.

Forest Terror

The two brothers were in knee-deep snow as they trudged through the northern forest. The pair were supposed to be hunting by daylight only, but the brothers knew that nobody would say boo if they were caught after dark. There were more deer in these woods than there were people within a hundred miles. And it wasn't like they were purposefully hunting by night.

They should have been settled in the tent group, cooking up some grub on the camping stove. Unfortunately, that wasn't to be as Colin, the younger brother, was quite possibly the world's worst map and compass navigator. He'd shot a bearing during the last bit of daylight that took the pair about a mile from where they were supposed to be.

It became dark and the full moon rose high above the trees.

Danny, the older brother by ten years took it in stride. There was rum in the sled. They'd be bedding down in a surplus army tent designed for winter. Between the two-burner stove and lantern with spare mantles, they could heat the tent and dry their wet mittens and felt insoles for the morning trek back to the pickup and possibly a deer while on route if they were lucky.

"It's dark enough, Colin," said the older brother. "Let's set up camp and bed down for the night. We'll give it a go once more at first light. Deer will be active around dawn anyhow. If we wind up shooting a charging moose, I have no idea how we could get it out of the bush. Probably have to butcher it in the snow and take the biggest pieces back with us on the toboggan."

Colin nodded. "Sounds good to me. Maybe come morning I can figure out where the hell we are on the map."

Danny patted his younger brother on the shoulder. "I'll show you a trick tomorrow that will pinpoint where we are on the map. A three-point resection. I'll teach you how to do it and you'll see, it's easy after a few tries. If your map is accurate and you know how to read the ground, it's impossible to get lost."

Young Colin heaved a weary sigh and looked around for a flat area inside the tree line to pitch the tent. He found one after a few seconds and started stamping the snow flat beneath his winter boots. "This looks pretty good," he said, pointing down to the ground in front of his feet.

"Let's get moving then," said the older brother.

It took twice as long as it normally took to pitch the tent, to carpet the floor with pine boughs, and to bury the flaps in the fresh snow. Their rifles had to be left outside the tent as they would collect condensation going from ten below outside to around two or three degrees inside the tent. By nine at night, they were cooking up a very late supper on the stove. Danny poured his brother a cupful of hot water from the pot on the stove into which Colin deposited a pouch of instant coffee.

Sorry about going off target," the younger brother said as he swished the coffee around inside his tin cup.

"Don't worry about it," said the older brother, now dumping

a cloth bag of chopped potatoes, onions, and bologna into an aluminum frying pan. "We'll retrace our steps in the snow. It'll be an easier trek back as we won't have to break trail any longer."

Colin nodded. "That will be nice. Hopefully, we don't get any snow overnight. Don't want to bury our footprints."

The older brother stirred the contents of the frying pan off and on for about ten minutes; until everything was tender. Outside, the full moon shone clear and deadly on the forest. One could easily hear the whoosh of the icy north wind rolling through the treetops high above the tent. The pair devoured their meal after a day of hauling the toboggan through the back forty.

Next, they shared a few shots of rum. It burned all the way down and neither brother was complaining. The temperature would drop to -20 Celsius overnight as it often did in November on those years when winter came early and stayed late.

Danny poured himself a cup of hot water and made some coffee. He lit a cigarette and watched his younger brother pull his sleeping bag out of its valise. Colin never joined up to serve choosing instead to apprentice as a heavy-duty mechanic. It was a good place for him to be, the older brother noted to himself. The kid would never be out of work.

"I'll do stove watch for the first couple of hours," said Danny. "Then we'll switch. We keep that stove and lantern going all night so we both need to make sure their tanks are filled with naphtha before the next guy goes on shift."

Colin snorted. "That sounds like the way you would do it in the army. You are on leave you know."

The older brother chuckled mildly. "Yeah, I guess that's pretty much how they do it in the army."

"It's all very ordered-sounding," said Colin. "And it makes perfect sense, so I guess I've learned a little bit of ... what do you call it again? Forest ... field ..."

"Field craft," Danny said. "Once you've got field craft mastered you can handle pretty much anything."

Fate chose that moment. A wild, unnatural sounding howl echoed through the forest. Loud, guttural, commanding. It demanded the attention of all living things within earshot. Tonight, was the hunt, and the werewolf was hungry.

"That's no wolf, Danny," Colin lowered his voice.

"Pretty sure you're right," his brother replied sounding dead serious. "Get dressed and then dim the lantern."

"W-What are you going to do?"

"I'm going to get my rifle and ready and take the SOB down," he said, business-like. Decisive. The way a good section commander should. "So are you, get your shit on and get outside ASAP. Follow my lead and we should be okay.

Colin quickly dressed himself and then killed the stove and lantern. The brothers unzipped the front flap when the ungodly howling started up again. This time much louder and closer.

"Change of plans," said Danny as he grabbed his brother's rifle and tossed it to him. "Whatever the hell that noise is, I don't want to stick around to find out what it came from. We'll follow the trail back."

Colin could feel the tension in his brother's voice amid the howling that was getting closer and closer.

"No time," the younger brother choked. "Whatever it is, let's shoot the damned thing if we get a bead on it."

Both brothers cocked their weapons and sat back-to-back in the snow. It was the closest thing to an all-round defense given the circumstances. Something big was coming, they could hear it crashing through the woods. The pair brought their rifles to their shoulders just as an enormous beastly silhouette appeared at the edge of the forest.

"H-Holy shit, what the hell is that? A kind of bear?" Danny whispered. The creature could hear every syllable and vowel of the brother's discussion. It could hear them from miles away. It picked up their scent from even further away.

The monster was just twenty meters away and the next moment it was diving for the older brother. Danny fired three shots at the wolf as it flew like a missile. Two missed their target, one hit the creature in the chest. It tumbled clumsily into a roll as it landed and then got back to its feet easily. The growl, menacing, terrifying. Fight or flight? But how can you fight something that shouldn't exist, thought the younger brother.

He took aim and fired a shot that hit the beast in the shoulder. It was the last thing Colin ever did. The monster's wound healed up in as much time as it took for the werewolf to break into a blindingly fast run right at the young man.

Danny fired two shots, missing by a country just as the creature's claws slashed Colin's belly. The younger brother's insides spilled onto blood-soaked snow. The older brother broke into a run, then quickly spun around, and fired another two rounds at the werewolf. The monster lifted its head from its prize, its face red with Colin's blood. It emitted a sniff as another two shots missed, thumping into the ground next to the beast.

"Shit, shit, shit, shit, shit," the older brother cursed as he quickly reloaded his rifle. The werewolf abandoned its prey and went straight for him. Danny fired two quick shots, this time hitting their mark, but it wasn't enough to stop the beast. Driven by supernatural hunger, the creature stood up to its full height, towering over its terrified prey. It let out a deadly snarl as it struck. Lashing out with its lethal claws, striking off Danny's head in a single blow. It started digging through the dead man's chest. Ripping out chunks of flesh and scattering it in all directions.

In the distance, the sound of snow machines. The werewolf snuffed and continued feeding while the mechanical noise was echoing through the woods, louder and louder every few seconds. It didn't take long for headlights to appear in the woods near the creature and its fresh kills. This time the werewolf reared up to get a better look. It sniffed the foul-smelling winter breeze as it carried the stench of engine exhaust, but it could smell the blood, the warm flesh of three people. The beast charged, kicking up snow and frozen turf in its bloody wake.

Three snow machines. Three new sources of prey and it wasn't even halfway through the night yet. The first victim, a man in an orange snow suit. He went down amid a roar from the creature, face slashed so hard it tore off his lower jaw. The snow machine continued driverless until it smashed into a tree and caught on fire. Fingers of orange flame lit up the darkness as the werewolf went after the remaining two snow machines that were racing away from the carnage.

To the werewolf, it was fresh meat time. It bolted after another machine as it blew through the wood line and entered a clearing with deep powdery snow. The sleds might have been fast, but the wolf was just as fast in snatching a rider by the left arm. It easily pulled the driver off the sled and then tore off the man's arm. Blood spurted onto the snow as the wolf buried its face in the man's neck and pulled out his throat.

The last sled crashed through snowdrifts and collided with a snow-covered boulder sticking out like a henge. The snow machine exploded in a bright fireball, taking its rider with it. This had been a good night for the wolf. A full belly, it stepped carefree through the bloody carnage.

Dawn came late in the dead of winter. The wolf could have continued hunting and instead, it wandered through the forest, following its nose to its lair. A safe place to rest. The creature sniffed and lay down on its side. It fell asleep.

The man inside the monster woke up shivering as he always did when the changes happened in the winter. He'd dug the lair two seasons ago. He'd put pine boughs on the ground. He'd prepared a change of clothing inside a metal box along with a half-bottle of whisky to warm his insides. It didn't take long to dress though the clothing was the same temperature as the winter. He shivered mercilessly as he pulled up his trousers and zipped the fly. Next was a thick cable knit sweater and a pair of winter boots with felt insoles.

The man took three serious slugs of whisky and placed the bottle back in the metal box. He continued to shiver, driving his hands into his pockets as he ran through the forest to the place where he'd parked his car. Just as he had done each month for the past two years. The spare key was in a metal box with a magnetic bottom, just inside the front left wheel well. He opened the door with the key and climbed inside. His car started easily given the cold night. It took about ten minutes for the heat to kick in.

He backed out and put the car in drive, taking one last look around. There was too much carnage too close to his lair this time. There would be police. It was time to find a new lair. He had twenty-seven days to do it. He pulled into a coffee shop drive thru as he entered town. He bought a large coffee and a couple of donuts. He parked the car and took a swig of the hot coffee. Then he took a bite out of a donut and looked at himself in the rear-view mirror.

"Twenty-seven days to find a new lair," he said between chews. "Need to get farther away from town this time. I don't feel guilt. None. I am what I have become, and I am alive. I have no intention of dying anytime soon."

He put the car in drive and headed out on the highway. Fifty miles this time. Fifty miles and maybe there wouldn't be any more people to kill. Just livestock and deer. More than enough to feed his monster.

I wonder if I should give it a name?" he said, as his car disappeared down the road.

Whistler Mountain Werewolf

"I scraped and worked and begged my way all over the country during the depression. Sometimes, but not often a man had some rare good luck when it came to finding a job.

In most cases there was very little work. So, we men would hop a box car and ride from Winnipeg all the way to the west coast. I jumped off the train and thumbed a ride to Whistler Mountain, an hour north of Vancouver. Turned out the driver of the small truck was the foreman of a survey crew and he offered me a job for a couple of days. Of course, I said yes even though I didn't know a thing about surveying. It turned out all I had to do was hold a pole in the ground while the real surveyor did the hard work. I just had to move the pole wherever the surveyor told me.

Now, nobody just fell into a job like that in those days. I remember saying 'this better not be a racket.'

Make work. Out in the sticks. An outdoor camp with tents and showers and a mess tent. Run by veterans of the great war. Manual labor that paid very little. Nobody wants to live in boot camp, and that's what the government was doing, see?

The monster. It's even hard to believe what I saw eighty years later because it was so awful. I hid myself as soon as the thing began its bloody rampage. A supply tent was where the carnage began. At first, I didn't want to believe what I was seeing could be real. It just couldn't possibly be real. My God, it leaped onto one poor man who wasn't fast enough. I'm sure he didn't even know what hit him he was dead so quickly. It snapped his neck with its powerful teeth and then it began ripping into his shoulder.

I couldn't help them. What could anyone do against such ferocity? It was much more than just a huge dog. It was a demon from the pits of you-know-where with a taste for human flesh. Powerful muscles covered by a veil of greying fur. Thick and bushy at the monster's shoulders. Pointy ears that could home in on even the tiniest whisper.

The dying man's screaming roused other men from their tents and that's when the bloodbath began in earnest. Some grabbed their shovels, sledges, and axes as they went after the creature intent on killing it. They might well have been successful if the group of ten men had a few guns between them. They made a circle around the beast, their digging tools anchored into the ground like the ancient Spartans.

I still feel like a coward because I wasn't out there with those men. But had I not been hiding I wouldn't be here to tell the story. Those men didn't stand a bloody chance, it was so fast. It ripped through them slashing and tearing at their faces and necks. Two more men's heads were torn off. Blood splattered and splashed every which-way. Organs were torn out of each body and cast aside like rotting garbage.

The screaming haunts me to this day. Each man must have known he was done for, but it didn't stop them from crying out in pain. Some called for their mothers or fathers. Ten men, dead in less than three minutes.

I remember whispering 'full moon' as I watched the monster head up a trail to the administrative tent where the old soldiers were bunked. The door burst open as the werewolf was about to tear into the canvas. Three men started blasting with their rifles.

Blam! CLICK CLACK. Blam! CLICK CLACK Blam! When one man fired two men were reloading or ready to continue blasting at the creature. We knew there were firearms on site, you see. Everybody knew it. We were in the sticks and there were bears and wolves and cougars aplenty at that time. It felt like we were under guard sometimes. For those survivors of that terrible night, each had to be damned grateful to those ex-sergeants and officers who kept their heads when the monster attacked them.

The wolf lay on its side for about ten or twenty seconds. The it raised itself up on its back legs and leaped like a coiled spring. The old soldiers fired at the creature again. *Blam! CLICK CLACK. Blam! CLICK CLACK Blam! Blam! CLICK CLACK. Blam! CLICK CLACK Blam!*

I lost count of how many bullets slammed into that beast. I know it was a hell of a lot. Ten men butchered by a hell hound. That's what I think werewolves are. I've had decades to think on it. But yes, I believe that werewolves are hell hounds come to life in our world for one night each month We need to learn a hell of a lot more about the beasts.

That night the full moon shone on our camp at the base of Whistler Mountain like a spotlight. It was as if the night wanted to watch the carnage and it asked the moon to run the light show. The men kept reloading and shooting, bullets tearing into the monster's flesh in loud thumps. It tumbled over a large stone sticking out of the ground and the men fired two more volleys. They killed the hell out of that thing. But more horror was to come as the dead creature began to slowly transform into a human being. The creature's flesh just fell off in chunks and dissolved like sugar in water.

I left the tent, my hands and legs shaking. I tried not to look at the blood-stained ground and the body parts scattered here and there, but it was hard not to see that kind of thing. I caught up with the old sergeants as they poked at the dead man with the muzzles of their weapons.

"'It was a bear that killed all these men, see?" said one of the sergeants. A big man who looked like he might have wrestled bears for a living at some point in the past. "The dead guy is just another victim. He got caught in the crossfire after using the outhouse. That's what the story will be."

Nobody argued. I don't believe there has been a werewolf attack or sighting in that area since that awful, awful night."

CHAPTER 11: WEREWOLF WHISTLE-BLOWERS

Throughout this book, numerous interviewees have talked about disappearing evidence that proves werewolves are real. That government would wish to hide anything that might cause a population-wide panic. It's one of the reasons why some nations have developed legislation that targets whistle blowers. Many of these laws are wrapped up in the guise of protecting national security. Are werewolves a national security threat? Let's be realistic: Unless someone has fashioned a werewolf mind control device, I wouldn't expect an invasion any time soon.

All that said, there is a legitimate concern about public safety. If monsters walk the earth and human beings are at the top of their menu, then yes, steps should be taken. If government were to acknowledge the werewolf phenomenon, the resources of government could be enacted to educate citizens about the threat. Most of the whistle-blowers I talked with said they would do it all again because of the public's right-to-know. I must agree with them: we're not at war and nobody has invoked emergency powers. Risk to public health is another aspect of protecting citizens that whistle-blowers acknowledge is a significant factor that needs to be considered.

It's almost as if the authorities want the phenomenon to look like it is supermarket tabloid worthy because then the threat of werewolves can be laughed at. The fact is that some fairy tales are quite real. The Big Bad Wolf comes once each month, only he won't blow your house down. Instead, he will crash through the bay window and butcher every living thing inside. That is the kind of information the public needs to know.

Coordination Between Levels of Government

"I wouldn't say that the werewolf phenomenon is a topic that is constantly top of mind for local, provincial and federal authorities. It's not even on their collective radar. That's not to discount the merciless nature of werewolf attacks and the impact on victim's families or those who survive an attack. It's just that we don't have large numbers of werewolves running amok — obviously, they don't run in packs.

The challenge when trying to coordinate levels of government on a subject that relates to public safety is to get consistency. That simply doesn't exist and won't until there is an army of werewolves working for one of Canada's enemies.

I'm a senior civil servant. I won't tell you which level of government, but I've seen it all. I've heard it all. There is no secret government organization whose purpose is to disappear evidence of werewolves. That is strictly tin-foil hat stuff. Canada's governments are terrible at keeping secrets. They're territorial and protectionist and don't like to play nice with other parts of the country.

You would have to establish and somehow maintain top secret operations along the lines of the Manhattan Project to really keep a secret. And even then, it's just not feasible. Even the Manhattan Project had spies. A lot easier to redact things with a cheap black marker you can get at the dollar store.

Other evidence? The shredder. See? Easy. Does government have a special operations branch to deal with things that go bump in the night? Absolutely not. Governments typically deny the existence of werewolves in the same manner they deny information at a news conference: with bafflegab and deflection.

That's a learned skill. Nobody outside of government communicates in the same manner as they do. I'll close by saying that inter-provincial coordination is near impossible to establish because of regional pissing matches. That's the Canadian way.

Secret Servers

"There is no branch of government that would ever have something on record: like the existence of a top-secret intelligence department that deals with supernatural threats.

That, to my knowledge doesn't exist but I could be wrong. It's not something G20 nations would ever admit to. What they do have are secret servers. Acres of secret computer servers. Empty office space for example. They're huge and can physically secured from outsiders. Hackers would be a different story, obviously.

I know where I work, they had the military send in their own computer techs to do the installation of so many miles and miles of cables and machines. It's locked up tight and you can only get it if you have been bio-marked. I know this because I still work there. For how much longer? Who knows, really. One thing is certain, they will eventually learn that it was me who dropped the 2 GB of CCTV data showing a werewolf utterly shredding a bouncer at a nightclub on Queen Street in Toronto. It ran up the damned wall of the building after it was done. Disappeared on the roof. That's where the footage ends. It was in the news, about five years ago. They sold it as a nutjob attack which it wasn't.

You've seen the footage. Lots of people have. *(Author's Note: I nod at him.)* It is impossible to fake what you've seen. What thousands have now seen. Government PR types go on high alert. But so far, nothing has taken with the public's imagination because it's very hard to unsee what you have seen. Maybe they are still processing it.

I suspect that leaked material would have more credibility if there was more than cursory news coverage of the leak. It hasn't been on the ten o'clock news, so to speak. So, it's not getting the coverage which would lend credibility to the footage. We're still in 'Bigfoot is a myth' territory. Incidentally that creature might be the only thing in the forest a werewolf would be wise to steer clear of.

Yes, I've seen footage of Bigfoot. There's not just one of them. There are families of them, and they're so far hidden in the woods you need special technology if you have a hope. That technology exists. It's called thermal imagery. Is there recorded thermal imagery of Bigfoot? I can't see why not. Secret servers. Machine learning. That's really what needs to be investigated.

What the government knows but won't tell us. Forget about

werewolves. As a side, don't want to get attacked by a werewolf? Easy. Stay home when there is a full moon."

Nobody Has the Final Say in How to Obfuscate

"I'm a career civil servant. I've seen it all, and one disturbing trend is for government's ability to obfuscate and to give non-answers to important questions of policy. Understand, it's a dance between the press and politicians because nobody answers a question the way a politician does. It's an extension of the overall bureaucrat speak that frustrates many people. Could you imagine explaining a werewolf attack in bureaucrat speak? If there's been an attack in your town, chances are you've already heard it.

Nobody has the final say in how to obfuscate. Some politicians are born with the ability and others develop it over time. The hopeless ones have their lines given to them before a presser.

You either believe these things are real or you don't. I choose to believe. There are politicians in Ottawa who believe in the phenomenon as well. Everybody has a story, but nobody will come forward to publicly state what they know. It's the political and bureaucratic equivalent of pulling the blanket over your eyes when you hear something go bump in the night.

The reasons nobody has the final say on this topic is because the mindset, I believe, is see no evil, hear no evil. Anybody reading this who has dealt with government knows a bit about the frustrating bureaucratic wall they must climb. That's not to say the authorities don't have evidence of werewolves in their possession. They do. I've seen it. I know where they store it along with bushels of other items, they don't want the public to know about. I would tell you but The Official Secrets Act still applies to retirees.

If you've had trouble finding the point of my sharing of experiences relating to the so-called phenomenon of werewolves, that's the entire point. Word salad? Reframed phraseology. You know, after all my years attending government pressers it still amazes me how members of the news media don't call politicians on their bureaucrat speak. It just never happens.

Because nobody has the final say, it makes it much harder to hold authorities accountable for their obfuscation. Nobody in their right mind is going to step up to the microphone at a presser and say, "the grisly discovery this morning points to a werewolf attack." That would be three miles past the 'dumbest thing you could ever say' department."

Werewolf Weaponization

"I leaked the intelligence brief, and it didn't even make a fart in the news cycle. I even leaked it on a Monday morning so as not to have the story wind up getting buried by weekend news. It's hard enough to believe in monsters let along believe that our enemies are experimenting in weaponizing the creatures.

(Author's Note: he hands me the brief. It looks like the real deal.)

The military industrial complex is a living thing. If it says werewolf weaponization is the way things are going then you can be certain that's where it's all going. The brief assesses the threat of werewolves as being marginal but when observing through a tactical lens that's something else entirely.

I have no idea how it would work. I have no clue what different countries might be up to. I don't even know what our own country is up to. The brief is legitimate. You will see the names of deputy ministers and senior bureaucrats on the distribution list. I've contacted every name on the list and nobody has returned a call or an email. It makes one think that something fishy is going on.

Article three of the brief is particularly disturbing. A Soviet-era top secret project to provide a so-called 'werewolf assets' to units all the way down to company level. Small unit deployment around full-moon cycles. No idea what size assets they are talking about, but the brief is filled with code words like that.

At first glance I thought, 'this is pure bullshit'. Then I remembered there hasn't been a weapon made yet that mankind hasn't used in wartime. Might as well add werewolves to that list of weapons. I have no idea just what is involved in weaponizing werewolves, but the fact that it was even being discussed as the leaked material shows, is disturbing. And still, no media interest in the story. Not even a whisper.

About the only thing that might grab their attention would be a politician turning into a hairy monster during a government announcement for a new national park or something along those lines."

Intimidation Tactics

"I have acquired evidence of government tampering with the truth about the werewolf phenomenon. Much of what I have done is to have applied the Freedom of Information Act. Dozens of requests. From multiple departments. From Government Services and Infrastructure Canada to National Defence all the way to Justice.

I started getting phone calls and text messages. I've saved them all. Just blank text from a number with an area code that keeps changing with each text. None of the area codes are Canadian. Same thing with the phone calls. Different area codes and numbers. No message. Just a click from their end on my voicemail.

Yes, we all get spam calls and texts and emails. But not five or six a day. I would normally get five or six in a week. I was going to make a complaint but there's nothing one can do other than to put the numbers on the national do not call list. The one that does not work and never had from day one. I don't believe the requests that I have made are anything more explosive than other freedom of information requests from other people. We have a right as citizens to know what our government gets up to.

I have also been followed on four separate occasions in the last six months. Same car each time. I've reported the license number which always comes up as having been stolen. You know, there isn't a hell of a lot of help from the authorities on this kind of harassment. The mere fact that little old me, a man who works in the service department at a car dealership, I might add. What kind of threat to government secrecy am I. I'm nobody.

Except I'm not a nobody. I can't track how many werewolf attacks there are in Canada, the United States ... basically anywhere. That's why I was making some freedom of information requests. Why send people to follow me on something that nobody believes in? And guess what? There are other people in Canada and overseas who have reported the same kinds of incidents as I have experienced. Not every case deal with werewolves. From how much a member of parliament spends on coffee each month to requests dealing with the federal budget. You name it."

The Fake Transformation Video

"I'm the one who recorded the so-called fake transformation video that wound up on the local news here in Victoria. It made the news in Vancouver too, but that's as far as things went from the traditional news media. I'm surprised it was even mentioned. This was much more frightening than mysterious lights in the sky that may or may not be visitors from another planet.

A man turned into a monster in the front seat of his SUV. I hope to God I never see anything like it again. Five minutes of footage from my parked car. I couldn't not record it on my phone. And the news, by the way, only showed a few seconds of the transformation. I mean, obviously they couldn't show the full five minutes. The papers didn't pick the story up, so I think this was just a one-off.

All I was doing in that mostly empty parking lot outside the coffee shop was, ta-da, enjoying a cup of coffee on my way to work on the night shift. I had just quit smoking and was passing the coffee and donut test. That's not too much to ask, right?

I don't normally pull my phone out to record perfect strangers in their cars. This was different. At first, I thought the man was having a seizure and that's why I grabbed my phone. To call 911. I froze when I saw him tear off his shirt. Fur was growing all over his body. Of course, I pressed record. I watched in horror as he dug his fingers into the dashboard and his forearms twisted grotesquely into a pair of fur covered front legs. Then I saw his fingers stretch in length and he started tearing at the dashboard with newfound claws. I zoomed on most of the transformation. All they showed on the news was a 'vicious dog' accidentally locked in a car along with a reminder that even at night, you should never lock Spot in the wagon.

Please. That just insults one's intelligence. I think the reason they reported it was because the video was so graphic that it was going to wind up online anyway. I also believe that you must be a complete dolt to think there aren't other videos of the same thing. So, here's the real reason I think the powers that be are trying to put the big scare on me. Ready? I think they're counting on me being scared enough to keep my mouth shut about what I saw that night.

I expect to wind up getting audited any day now. It's a kind of administrative reprisal that can only come from the top. Civil servants aren't in the business of screwing people around. The fact is the new approach is to simply deny and discredit. About that fake transformation video? Well, it's fake news, isn't it? You can just say it's fake news and enough of the population already buys into that.

That night in the parking lot introduced me to the concept of stone-cold terror. The monster tore up the inside of that car and then smashed its way through the rear window. It was huge and I wasn't sticking around. I tore out of that parking lot and the werewolf gave chase. I thought for sure, that if the monster could smash its way out of an SUV, it could easily smash its way in to my little compact. I floored it, driving up the street at about seventy kilometers an hour. I hit 911 again and said there was a huge wolf chasing my car up the boulevard. I hung up and kept bombing up the road and I was putting distance between me and the monster.

I heard sirens. They took my call seriously. In seconds there were red and blue flashing lights in my rearview mirror. I didn't stick around to see what happened. The next day the morning news said the police had put down a large wolf that somehow made it into the north industrial section. They explained it away just like that. People believed them. The rest is where I'm at right now. I'm labeled a conspiracy theorist. Tin foil hat kind of man."

CHAPTER 12: KING OF THE MOONLIGHT

I have included a final short story in this volume. Penned by a journalist who is also host to the creature after being attacked while covering a series of grisly killings in Northern Alberta. Each killing ghastlier than the next with partially eaten victims found frozen to the ground or worse, ripped to pieces with no hope of recovering the entire body.

He'd managed to record a transformation on a small helmet camera hidden in a corner of a ceiling beam. It was more of a crawlspace than anything. An abandoned farmhouse in the middle of a field about fifty miles from nowhere. Far enough away, he'd hoped because his creature had already killed seven in two transformations that made the news due to their savagery. Donning a facemask covering his nose and mouth, he began chasing out the mice and sweeping out decades of dust and cobwebs in preparation.

It wasn't the most secure place to contain a transformation, but it was better than running amok in the city. That's what they were calling it now, wasn't it? Containment?

The supernatural. It wasn't supposed to be real and yet he was host to a creature he didn't believe in until it happened to him. He replayed that moment over again each day, how he came to become a monster. How his study habits that introduced him to the creature that changed his life. Late night at the library. A warm late autumn breeze. He thought he might stop off at the pizza joint and grab a slice. A suitable reward for an honest day's research.

He remembered his stomach rumbled loudly as he waved at a group of four stumbling across the pitch on the way home from the pub, no doubt. At least they didn't drive anywhere. He spotted another group of three students chattering amiably as they crossed the southwest corner of the pitch.

The howl came as the full moon appeared, splashing its cool blue light. Screaming began about twenty seconds later. He remembered how he ran for his life after he saw what was causing the screaming. Huge, feral, and hungry. It slashed and tore its way through the group at the southwest corner, standing its full height. Towering over its prey. They screamed and wailed for God and their mothers to save them as the wolf ripped them apart.

But it wasn't done yet.

He remembered a great weight crashing into his back like a wrecking ball and sending him tumbling. He rolled to a stop face-first in the wet grass when the monster stepped onto his back and started tearing apart the thick canvas backpack to get to the sweet fleshy bits. It swiped his back so hard the student spun around like a cat toy. Its claws tore through his thick denim jacket in two or three places. Enough to bleed just as easily as all the rest of the prey it had taken that night.

The anthropology student felt blood trickling down his back and across his chest. He got back to his feet and stumbled across the pitch and into the parking lot adjacent. More horrible screaming and pleading to a higher power echoed through the night. The last thing he remembered before going into shock was crashing through the doors at the campus security post

He opened his eyes in the hospital. He looked down to see the bandage wrapped around his chest and over his shoulder. He sat in his bed with his knees up against his scarred chest. He imagined the monster was a thinking beast, but not much beyond the need to feed its supernatural hunger. "It's not my fault. I'm not a killer."

The death toll since his first transformation suggested otherwise.

He watched as he did nearly every day after that first transformation. He treated the video with clinical observation one would expect from an anthropologist major. He timed from the moment he first cried out that his body was on fire to the completed transformation: twenty-one minutes and fifteen seconds. It was as if the moon had snapped its fingers, ordering the metamorphosis to begin at once.

The terrible noise of fresh bones cracking and snapping. Screams of his immeasurable torture. That was how he recorded it in a notebook filled with scribbles and question marks. He narrowed his eyes and leaned in to watch the transformation for what seemed like the millionth time.

He maximized the media player just as his spine popped loudly. He watched on, still in stunned silence as the screen showed a man in unspeakable pain. Whose ankles cracked, ground, and stretched, raising him up nearly two feet from his normal height of five feet and eleven inches. His arms began reshaping into long, muscular forelegs. Thick black fur appeared through the pores in his skin as he fell onto all fours.

The student winced as hair sprouted from a back and torso that was stretching and twisting into a large chested beast with a narrow waist. Front claws, larger than anything the student had seen on any mammal. One moment there were two adult male hands and the next few moments a set of deadly claws with nails at least three or four inches long.

The wolf's legs and torso continued to sprout fur. A wolf's tail and ears extending up from the sides of a skull that had transformed into that of a large canine predator. Nose, upper and lower jaw appeared as the human skin peeled back to reveal its newly formed muzzle. Human teeth fell out of its mouth and onto the dirt floor as a set of sharp white teeth grew grotesquely into the man-wolf's mouth. A fleshy tearing sound was the last of the transformation as the remainder of the skin of his human face fell to the floor with a squishy sounding plop.

He stopped the media player and touched his face with his fingertips. "This is my life now," he said to the screen. "I'm fucked."

He wasn't wrong. And what was the point of studying anthropology when you become a monster for one night a month? What was the point of any of it?

His inner voice. An entity he'd spent much of his life ignoring finally got the student's attention.

We are what we are now. That's it. Do you understand? We are now what we become every month during a full moon. There is no changing that.

There is little need to speculate on the reasons why werewolves exist when you're hosting the monster. There might be some value in understanding the creature more so that in time, there might be a way to control it subconsciously. We must live a life in isolation. We are innocent of murder because of what we become through no fault of our own. They will shoot us dead if they see the monster. There is no question on that.

"I have a right to live," he said as he closed the screen on his laptop. "Those people my creature killed had a right to live. What point is there in giving a life in atonement for a life taken when I simply was not there?"

It would be, he knew, a stretch for anyone to believe that he wasn't somehow criminally responsible for death by werewolf. The savagery of the killings alone would be more than enough to flip the human need for retribution. In the old movies, peasants didn't come after monsters with pitch forks and burning torches because they wanted to give monsters a big comfy hug. They wanted to burn the damned thing at the stake if they could. They wanted it dead.

"That isn't going to be me," said the student as he gazed out the window into the night sky. The next full moon would be in five nights. Not enough time to somehow find a magical cure to his condition but more than enough time to take more security precautions. He wasn't a practicing Catholic, but he decided to make sure he was wearing his St. Christopher's medallion during the night of the change. He may have been the patron saint of travelers, but crucifixes were, presumably, for vampires. He was counting on the silver and the power of Him to maybe combine forces and send his werewolf packing.

Even though no evidence existed for silver ever working on a werewolf the silver in the medal couldn't hurt. He spent the next day online as he continued his search for sources of werewolf mythology. Perhaps he would find something useful.

"Possession by a demon? Not the last time I checked," he said to the screen. "A curse thrown at by a loved one with a smile on their face. I need a loved one for that to happen."

His search continued until he fell asleep.

He woke up to the sound of nearby police sirens and maybe even a fire truck. He climbed out of bed and pulled open the sliding door to the balcony. He saw the fiery glow coming from a pair of crashed automobiles at the intersection about two blocks away. Emergency vehicles pulled up to the scene and began the business of putting out the fires from both vehicles.

"Holy shit," he said as he watched both vehicles become engulfed in flames. The smell of burning rubber wafted up the twelve floors of the building where he lived. Burning rubber and seared human flesh. And the screaming of those caught in the flames.

He nearly threw up over the balcony.

It wasn't a rescue mission. It was a cleanup. Six dead. Four in a minivan and two more dead in a beater sedan that didn't have any insurance.

He watched the flames in quiet fascination. He weighed the horror of burnt corpses inside an automobile against that of human beings found ripped apart and partially eaten. Burning people screamed and begged and called out to a higher power to save them. Just like people screamed and begged when the wolf had them. Manner of death was different, but the outcome was always the same. Pure horror.

"I'm no Talbot. Screw him," said the student as he slid back into bed and closed his eyes. "I'm no fucking monster in spite of what happens during the full moon."

The time came for the wolf to enter the night. The student pulled his beat-up car beside the abandoned farmhouse. The sun was still a few minutes from setting. He had the time to set up the camera in the cross beam just as before. He'd vowed to continue recording transformations. Only through research could there possibly be an answer for his mixed existence. Or maybe dumb luck. He'd take that too if he could.

He locked himself in the basement and climbed down the ladder. He'd disassembled the wooden stairs in the belief that he could trap the creature. As he climbed down the ladder, he wished he could be locked away in a bank safe for the night. If he had access to a safe it would be impossible for a werewolf to dig or smash its way out of it.

The door to the basement was fifteen feet to the floor. It was still possible for his wolf to get out but at least he was doing something. Farmland for miles around. Grid roads crisscrossed every few miles. Hopefully, he was far enough away from civilization when the monster finally managed to break free.

The fever hit within an hour of his arrival at the farmhouse. His screams went unanswered because he was muted inside the root cellar. Not that there was anyone for twenty miles in either direction. He fell onto the floor, the flashlight hanging from a beam by thick wire cast a yellow spotlight on the transformation.

His clothing off, the naked student fell onto all fours as the metamorphosis took firm hold. The light swung violently back and forth as the monster swiped at it. Its claws connected and the flashlight smashed against the wall and broke into pieces. It panted and began to pace in the darkness. No matter. The creature was born in the darkness. It lived because of the darkness and the power of the full moon.

And it wasn't going to be denied this night.

The wolf began to sniff about. The cellar smelled of damp and decay. But there was fresh air coming in. The beast rose to its full height as it stalked across the floor, following its nose to the fresh air. It stopped as it faced a cinder block wall. Above, however, was a door and freedom.

It jumped straight up with its powerful legs, and it swiped the wood of the door. Splinters flew in each direction as the creature kept jumping and slashing at the door. It wasn't long before there was a hole in the door big enough for the wolf. One last leap and it scrambled up the cinder block wall leaving huge gashes in the cement.

It pulled itself up and then through the door. Returning to all fours, the wolf raced out of the house and into the light of the full moon. It let loose with a single rapturous howl and then caught the scent of nearby prey. Off it went with supernatural speed. It tore across the field kicking up large clumps of dirt and clay.

The smell of meat. It was the only thing.

It followed its nose for five miles before it ran into the pack of wolves. They circled and bared their teeth at the creature. And the werewolf wasn't running anywhere. It went for the nearest wolf, slashing its way into its belly. It ripped the heart out of its prey and dropped the carcass it its feet. It let out a howl and the pack lowered their heads. The massive beast kicked dirt on its kill and then trotted away into the night. The pack followed close behind.

The werewolf.

King of the moonlight.

ACKNOWLEDGEMENTS

I've wanted to write this book for some time. And so, I wrote it in the middle of a pandemic. (I didn't try making sourdough as many did in the early days of lockdowns.) I love werewolves, always have. I had a Lon Chaney Wolfman model that glowed in the dark. It sat on my dresser for years as I grew up. Abbot and Costello meet Frankenstein? There's a wolfman in it? Yes please, I'd like to watch that very much.

It's not that I live and breathe werewolves, it's just that for me, they are the most interesting monster.

In my travels, I've met many a werewolf fan. And why not? Werewolves are scary as hell. My great thanks to award winning author Chadwick Ginther for his introduction to this book. He's a life- long werewolf fan and, I believe, had the same werewolf model I did. Thank you kindly, Chadwick.

Thanks to my wife, Cheryl, who is probably sick of hearing me talk about werewolves. Thank you to all werewolf fans who bought this book. I hope you enjoy. Now ... be mindful when the moon is full and something terrifying is howling in the near distance.

Best just stay in the house and lock the doors.

ABOUT THE AUTHOR

Sean Cummings

He's a multi-published author whose books range from the story of menacing poltergeists to the aftermath of the zombie apocalypse to a defrocked grim reaper who is just trying to get by in the human world. He lives in Saskatchewan with his wife, retired racing greyhound and an enormous spotted dog.

www.ingramcontent.com/pod-product-compliance
Lightning Source LLC
Chambersburg PA
CBHW022126170626
46808CB00002B/865